THE
FROLICSOME
CRYSTAL BALL

DAPHNE NEVILLE

ISBN: 9798378409358

PublishNation
www.publishnation.co.uk

Other Titles by This Author

Chapter One

Septuagenarian twin sisters, Hetty and Lottie, out for a walk with Hetty's dog Albert, in the early-May sunshine, were nearing the bottom of Long Lane when a large removal van swept along Pentrillick's main street. Quickening their pace, the trio reached the junction just in time to see the van turn left into the lane a short distance past the Crown and Anchor.

Hetty gasped. "That must mean the chap who has bought Saltwater House is in the throes of moving in at last. Come on, Lottie, let's follow it and see if we can spot him."

"What! No, Het, we can't, he might see us."

"But it doesn't matter if he does. I mean, he'll just think we're passing that way taking Albert for walkies."

"Woof," barked Albert on hearing his name.

"But isn't it a private road? I know we've been to the house before but we were invited then. I don't want to trespass."

"You won't because it's not. Just before the house, there's a bridleway which crosses the edge of a field leading down to the coastal path. Albert and I have been that way several times of late."

"Humph. No doubt hoping to see if there's any activity at Saltwater House."

"Of course and why not. Anyway, I'm sure you're just as curious as I am to see what he's like. All we know at present is that he's a retired gardener or something like that."

"And he's a bachelor," Lottie added, "That's about all Tess managed to wheedle out of the Goldworthys when the

1

sale was agreed. Although to be fair if the sale was managed by agents, the Goldworthys probably never even met him."

"Hmm, most likely but more to the point, if he's a bachelor I'd like to know why he's not been snapped up. I mean, if he were a widower or a divorcee I could understand him being alone but there can't be many chaps who reach retirement age without being wed."

"But you've never married, Het."

"No, but it's different with women. Anyway, I dedicated myself to my job. Midwifery's a very rewarding career, Lottie."

"And I daresay whatever he's called dedicated himself to gardening or whatever."

"Maybe. Anyway, come on, we're wasting valuable time."

The lane leading to Saltwater House was little more than a dirt track. Primroses, violets and bluebells grew in the shade of sycamore trees. Red campion and wild garlic flowered in profusion on the grass verges amongst towering cow parsley. When the trio reached a stile in the hedgerow beneath the white blossom of blackthorn, Hetty nodded to a signpost gleaming in the golden rays of the sun, pointing out the route of the footpath across the field towards the coastal path.

Lottie paused. "We shouldn't go any further than here, Het."

"But we're nearly there now. If you remember the track ends just round this next bend where the gates lead into the grounds."

"But we might be seen. I'd hate the new owner to think us nosy."

However, despite her objections, Lottie cautiously followed her sister around the last bend but to their dismay all they were able to see when they reached the open gates was the removal van which completely obscured the gravel path leading to the house. And because the vehicle faced the gates the sisters were unable to see the removal men or any of the new owner's possessions on board.

"Fiddlesticks!" Hetty was clearly very disappointed. "Still, never mind we'll pop to the pub tonight and see if anyone there knows any details."

"But it's Wednesday tomorrow and our turn to work in the charity shop. Remember we've agreed never to go the pub the night before we work unless there's a very good reason."

"Damn, yes, you're right, Lottie. On the other hand, I think we can claim finding out details of the village's latest newcomer *is* a very good reason."

Later, however, try as they might, the two ladies were unable to discover any fresh information regarding the new inhabitant at Saltwater House. Two people inside the Crown and Anchor acknowledged they had seen the removal van driving through the village but neither saw where it went. Furthermore, Tess Dobson, the one person who would be likely to know, had the evening off work.

"Ah Pickle, he might know something" gushed Hetty, as the aforementioned entered the bar and ordered a pint of cider. "I'll go and ask him."

Percy Pickering, known as Pickle, had been employed part-time to attend the gardens at Saltwater House by the previous owners, the Goldworthys. His nickname went back to when he was little; he couldn't say Pickering and so called himself Percy Pickling. That caused several people to call him young Pickling and gradually it was shortened to Pickle. A widower with grown up sons who had long since flown the nest, he lived alone in Hawthorn Road.

"All I can tell you," said Pickle, in answer to Hetty's question, "is that the new owner is likely to have me continue to pop in a couple of times a week just as before. That's what the estate agent said anyway but we'll have to wait and see. They have my details so fingers crossed the new chap will be in touch soon." Pickle took a sip of cider,

"I must admit I'll be devastated if he doesn't. I love the Saltwater gardens, you see. So quiet and peaceful up there and the views are stunning."

"Well, that's something," said Lottie, when Hetty relayed the news, "and hopefully the new chap will spend lots of time here and socialise with villagers, unlike the Goldworthys who seemed always to be away gallivanting somewhere or other."

For two days the sisters were unable to learn any more than they already knew about the retired gardener, but then on Friday morning, shortly after they had opened up the charity shop, a dark blue BMW pulled up alongside the pavement in front of the shop. After checking the coast was clear, the driver stepped from the car, hopped onto the pavement and opened the shop door.

"Good morning, ladies. I wonder if you'd be interested in a few bits and bobs I no longer have need for. I did intend to donate them to a charity shop back home but somehow the chore slipped my mind and the box has ended up here along with everything else."

For thirty seconds neither sister spoke. The man standing in the doorway had to be the new owner of Saltwater House yet he looked nothing like their mental picture. He was slim, six feet tall and had thick wavy silver hair parted to one side. He was clean-shaven, had twinkly blue eyes, and was immaculately dressed in a tweed jacket, beige chinos and fawn suede shoes. The nails on his beautifully clean hands were carefully manicured; a contrast to the hands of most gardeners.

"Yes, please," said Lottie finding her voice, "Donations are always welcome."

"Excellent. I'll go and grab them."

As he left the shop and opened up the boot of his car the two sisters looked at each other in wonder.

"Well," said Hetty, "that's a turn up for the book."

"If he's who we think he is, then, yes," Lottie agreed.

With a large cardboard box in his arms the stranger re-entered the shop. "Where shall I put it?"

"Oh, anywhere. On the floor perhaps," muttered Hetty.

He did as suggested and then rubbed his hands. "And may I ask the names of you ladies?"

"Of course, I'm Lottie," gushed Lottie, "and this is my twin sister, Hetty."

"Delighted to meet you, ladies," he shook their hands in turn, "and in case you're unaware, I'm the chap who moved into Saltwater House on Tuesday." He took a bow, "Layton Edgar Wolf at your service."

"And is there a Mrs Wolf?" Lottie asked, even though she knew there wasn't.

He laughed. "Sadly not. Clarence has never taken to any of my lady friends. At least not enough for me to share my life with them." He chuckled, "I always got the impression he was jealous."

"Clarence?" queried Hetty.

"My parrot. He's an African Grey and he's been with me for thirty-five years."

Lottie's jaw dropped. "An African Grey parrot. Does he talk a lot?"

"Oh, yes."

"I'd love to meet him."

"And so you shall. You see, I'm thinking of having an open house once I'm straight and then whoever wants to can call in for a coffee and introduce themselves. I'm keen to make new friends, you see, and when you get to my age time is of the essence."

"Oh, come on. You're not that old," blurted Hetty, beguiled by the scent of his aftershave.

"I'll be seventy-one in September, so hardly in the first flush of youth."

"Well, let us know if and when and we'll tell everyone we see," Lottie gushed enthusiasm, "Or better still we can put a notice in the shop window."

"Now that's a good idea. I'll print a few copies and drop one in to you when I've fixed a date."

"Ideal, and if we're not here you can leave it with Daisy or Maisie," said Hetty, "They do three days a week and so do we. On Sundays we're closed."

"Daisy and Maisie and Hetty and Lottie," chuckled Layton as he bade them farewell. "What delicious names you ladies have."

"Delicious!" gasped Lottie, as he pulled the shop door closed and stepped onto the pavement, "that sounds a bit sinister coming from the lips of a Mr Wolf."

Hetty chuckled, "I'm inclined to agree." She then knelt down to see what was in the box. "Hmm, clothes, and very nice too. I wonder why he no longer wants them."

"Maybe he fancied a change and has bought new stuff. On the other hand he might have put on a few pounds and they're on the tight side. There could be one hundred and one reasons."

"True, I suppose." Hetty picked up the box and took it out to the stockroom. "We'll deal with that later, meanwhile we need to decide whether or not to go to the pub tonight to spread the word of the coffee morning."

"Perhaps you ought to ask the crystal ball and it can decide for us."

"Excellent idea."

The crystal ball, as the ladies who worked in the charity shop liked to call it, had been amongst goods donated to the shop from a gift shop that had ceased trading. It was inside a box of colourful glass balls, the type once used by fishermen as floats for their nets. Each ball was encased in fine rope latticework, except for one, a single, clear glass ball tucked in the bottom of the box devoid of rope. Not sure what to do with it, Maisie and Daisy, working that day, placed it on the shop's counter and said for a bit of fun they'd treat it as a crystal ball.

"So what can you see?" Lottie asked as Hetty waved her hands over the glass orb.

"The mist, the mist is clearing and oh, I see two glasses of red wine."

"I thought you might."

Chapter Two

On Monday morning, Tess called in at the charity shop. In her hands she held three sheets of paper. "Something for you. Layton, the new Saltwater House chap, called into the pub last night and asked us to distribute these. He would have done it himself but he was pushed for time as he had to pop off up-country to his sister's for some reason or other. Anyway, they're posters for his coffee morning."

"Brilliant. When is it?" Hetty asked.

"Saturday the fourteenth of May. It'll be a drop in affair between ten and two." Tess handed a sheet of paper to Lottie.

"Who are the other notices for?" Hetty asked as she looked over her sister's shoulder and scanned the coffee morning details.

"The pasty shop and the village hall notice board. We have one in the pub too. James told Layton that other businesses would be happy to spread the word but he didn't want to be pushy, especially in places he's yet to visit."

"He's obviously been to the pasty shop then," reasoned Lottie.

"Yes, he appears to be very taken with Dolly and Eve's baking."

"And you say he's been in the pub as well," said Hetty, "Humph, we've not seen him in there."

"He's only been in a couple of times and they were both early evening visits and he didn't stay long."

"Oh, I see, that's how we'll have missed him then." Hetty looked puzzled. "He's not even been here for a week yet so I wonder why he's had to rush off up-country."

Tess shrugged her shoulders. "I might have heard wrong because I was taking a food order at the time, but I'm sure he said something to James about a parrot."

"That'll be Clarence," said Lottie, "Layton's African Grey. He must have left him with his sister while he moved down here."

On Thursday morning a car pulled up outside the sisters' home, Primrose Cottage. Lottie sitting at the table doing a crossword puzzle, glanced from the window and promptly leapt to her feet. "Debbie's back," she called to Hetty upstairs making her bed.

Hetty reached the bottom of the stairs just as Lottie opened the front door. Delighted to see their friend, the sisters hugged her in turn.

"Have I missed anything?" Debbie asked as they dragged her over the threshold.

Lottie closed the door. "You certainly have. Come in and sit down."

"And I'll make coffee," Hetty bustled off to the kitchen.

Debbie and her husband, Gideon, had been away from the village for a fortnight visiting Scotland to celebrate their ruby wedding anniversary. Originally they had planned a holiday abroad but not wanting to tempt fate regarding potential travel restrictions due to the Covid 19 pandemic affecting world travel, they opted to stay in the British Isles instead.

"So how was Scotland?" Lottie asked as they sat down side by side on the settee.

"Wonderful. The weather was kind and the scenery stunning. I never realised it was so beautiful and we've vowed to go again next year."

"Sounds lovely. Hugh and I went there many, many years ago before the children were born and we loved it too.

It was always our plan to go again when Hugh retired but, well, that wasn't to be."

"I am sorry. How long is it now since you lost your husband?"

"It'll soon be seven years." Lottie looked up as Hetty entered the room with mugs of coffee on a tray along with slices of fruit cake.

"Have you told Debbie about Layton yet?" Hetty asked.

"No, I was waiting for you to be here."

"Layton. Who's Layton?"

Hetty handed out the mugs of coffee and then between them they told all they knew about Layton Edgar Wolf.

"Has Kitty met him yet?" Debbie asked as the news sank in.

"No, sadly she's been laid up with the flu since just after you and Gideon went away so we've not been able to see her. We've told Tommy though and he's passed on the news."

"Oh dear. Poor Kitty. Poor you too. It must have been very frustrating not to have anyone to share the gossip with."

"It was," sighed Hetty, "We were actually tempted to message you even though you said not to make contact unless it was an emergency. Anyway, you're back now and Kitty is on the mend and hopefully will be well enough to go to the coffee morning. I assume you'll be there too, Debs."

"Of course. I wouldn't miss it for the world."

Lottie, a widow, had two grown up children. Bill was a supermarket manager who lived in the village with his wife Sandra at The Old Bakehouse, and Barbara who lived and worked in the United States. Bill and Sandra had three children: nineteen-year-old twins Kate and Vicki, both at university, and their older brother Zac, a plumber, who lived at Cobblestone Close, a relatively new housing estate, with his fiancée Emma. Zac and Emma were due to be married on September the third: a date brought forward by two weeks so that Barbara's partner could join her when she came over from America for the wedding.

On Friday the thirteenth, the day before the coffee morning, Bill came home from the supermarket where he worked. In his arms he held a cardboard box.

"I've a present for you," he kissed Sandra's cheek and placed the box on the dining room table.

"What is it?"

"Open it and see."

Carefully Sandra lifted the flaps. "A tortoise! Why on earth have you bought a tortoise?"

"I haven't. Bought him, that is. Terry, a chap I work with gave him to me. It belonged to his old mum, you see, but sadly she passed away a couple of weeks ago. Terry doesn't have a garden, just a small concreted back yard and so he asked if any of us would care to give him a new home. No-one volunteered so I said we'd have him."

"You old softy." Sandra gave Bill a quick hug. "But won't he eat your vegetables?"

"Given the chance he would but I'll put a gated picket fence around it to keep him out. I'll also make him a pen and we'll put him in it each night. Not that he can escape with walls all round and a solid back gate."

Sandra gently ran her hand over the tortoise's shell. "So what's he called?"

"Jim," chuckled Bill, "Terry's mum named him after her late husband who she claimed was very slow when it came to housework and especially washing up."

May the fourteenth was a warm and sunny day. Hetty and Lottie, both up early and looking forward to their visit to Saltwater House, discussed what to wear over breakfast.

"Listen to us," chuckled Hetty, "anyone would think we were going to Royal Ascot."

"Glad we're not. Coffee with Layton and meeting his parrot is much more up my street."

"I have to agree there."

Kitty, recovering from flu, and almost back to her normal self, left her home at the far end of Blackberry Way and called for her near neighbours, Hetty and Lottie en route. The three ladies left Primrose Cottage just before ten and at the bottom of Long Lane, sitting on a low wall by the entrance to the Crown and Anchor's car park, Debbie was waiting for them. Chattering away, they then made their way along the road until they reached the turning into the lane leading to Saltwater House.

"What's this lane called?" Lottie asked, "I assume it has a name."

"Short Lane," replied Kitty, who had lived in the village for her entire life.

Lottie chuckled, "Long Lane and Short Lane. I like that."

At the end of the lane, the gates into the grounds of Saltwater House were open to allow those who arrived by car to park their vehicles in front of the double garage. The ladies followed a gravel path which wound its way through shrubs and an array of small fir trees. At the end of the path, the house, large, detached and painted white, gleamed in the bright morning sunshine. They were not the first to arrive.

"Tess, you're here bright and early," said Hetty.

"That's because I'll not be able to stay long as I'm working this lunchtime, but I didn't want to miss out."

"Same with me." Beside Tess, sat Clara Bragg who worked as a cook at Pentrillick's care home for the elderly

"Where's our host?" Lottie asked.

"I'm here," Layton stepped out from the house with two mugs of coffee. He handed one each to Tess and Clara. He then shook hands with the ladies who introduced him to Debbie and Kitty.

"Wow, he's a handsome brute," whispered Debbie as Layton returned indoors for their coffee, "This parrot of his must be very influential for him to have remained single all these years. There must have been lots of women who'd have happily snapped him up."

"Where is Clarence?" Lottie sat down on one of the many garden chairs.

"Layton will bring him out to meet us all when there are more of us here," said Tess, "That's why he's bringing coffee out to us rather than we go indoors to collect it. At present, Clarence is in the kitchen along with George."

"George," said Hetty, "Who's George?"

"A Dachshund," giggled Clara, "He waddled out a few minutes ago, had a sniff around and then followed Layton back inside. I don't think he was very taken by us, was he Tess?"

"No, and from what we've heard I don't think the parrot will be too keen on us either."

The sound of gravel crunching informed them someone else was walking along the garden path. All heads turned to see retired Detective Inspector Paul Fox arrive. Paul lived in a flat above the village's pasty shop. With him was Jude Sharpe, partner of Eve Jones who ran the pasty shop along with her friend, Dolly Small.

"Paul, so glad you could make it," Hetty beckoned him to the vacant chair by her side, "You found us okay then."

"Well, it wasn't difficult and your directions were pretty comprehensive." He cast his eyes around the garden as he sat, "Nice place. Must be worth a fortune."

"Yes," said Lottie, "and the garden goes right down to the cliff edge."

"You've already had a look then."

"Not today, it was when we came here a few years back. Before Layton bought it this place belonged to the

Goldworthys, you see, and Mrs Goldworthy, I can't remember her Christian name, is the sister of someone who belonged to the drama group before Het and I moved here. Funnily enough his name was Paul too but he lives somewhere up-country now. Anyway, to do his sister a favour, he housesat for the summer while they were away, during which he invited all drama group members round for nibbles and drinks."

"Ah, a few males, at last," Layton emerged from the kitchen and handed out mugs of coffee to Hetty, Lottie, Debbie and Kitty. He then put down the tray and welcomed the two men.

Within an hour there were twenty-seven people standing and seated in the gardens of Saltwater House.

"Are you two an item?" Layton noticed Hetty and Paul chatting away in a world of their own.

Paul looked up, "Yes, I'm Hetty's toy boy," he teased.

Hetty slapped his thigh. "Cheeky. No, Layton, we're just good friends."

Paul pulled Hetty to her feet. "Come on Miss Tonkins. You can show me around the garden. That's if it's alright with Layton."

"Of course, please do. I'm very proud of the grounds even though I had nothing to do with their creation."

"Can I come too?" Clara asked, "Like you, Paul, I've not been here before and I might get some inspiration for the Pentrillick in Bloom Competition."

"Of course. The more the merrier."

With arms linked like characters in the Wizard of Oz following the yellow brick road, Paul, Hetty and Clara strode along the grass path which twisted and turned through spring flowers in deep attractive borders. The scent of lilac hung in the air but the flowers on a huge magnolia had gone over. At the end of the path a fountain sprinkled fine water into a small ornamental pond. Beyond the pond the garden sloped downhill and opened up into an area where plants and small shrubs lay nestled amongst the rocks that led down to a fence bordering the coastal path.

Meanwhile, back at the gathering, Lottie looked a little nervous. "Do you mind if I ask you a few questions, Layton? You see, we've all been led to believe that you're a retired gardener but your hands tell me otherwise."

Several heads nodded in agreement.

"Nearly right," Layton sat down, "In a nutshell I started out as a gardener but when the opportunity arose I bought a small run-down nursery with a bit of money left to me by my gran. I built it up, bought an adjoining field and opened it as a garden centre. It blossomed and became a very lucrative business. However, when I reached seventy I thought it was time to move on so I sold up and here I am."

As Hetty, Paul and Clara concluded their tour of the garden and returned to the others, Layton, having popped indoors came out with Clarence on his shoulder. The bird weighed up the crowd and then Layton said, "Clarence, call George." To the delight of the crowd, Clarence whistled and George ran from the house, tail wagging and stopped by the feet of Layton.

Meanwhile, at the Old Bakehouse, Bill who had the day off work, wondered if Tim the tortoise was as smart as Terry claimed. To test him, he decided to see if he could predict who would win the FA Cup Final at Wembley that afternoon. He had seen it done before with other animals, an octopus if he remembered correctly and there were numerous other creatures too. He set up the challenge by taking a lettuce from the fridge and placing leaves in two neat piles. Behind one he laid a blue pen to represent Chelsea, behind the other a red pencil for Liverpool. He then went in search of the tortoise which he found dosing in the sun beneath the washing line. Just as he stood the creature down several feet away from the lettuce, Sandra back from the care home where she worked part-time, stepped out into the garden.

"What are you doing, Bill?"

"Testing Tim to see if he knows who'll win the football. You never know, he might be psychic."

Smothering a smile, Sandra sat down on the lawn to see the outcome.

"Ah, Liverpool," said Bill gleefully, after a very long ten minutes. "Be cool if he's right."

Sandra stood up. "Well he has a fifty-fifty chance of being so."

Bill was not really into football, nevertheless curious to see if Tim was right he decided to watch the game, especially after Sandra hinted that the lawn needed cutting. The match went into extra time and was finally settled with a penalty shootout. Liverpool won and Tim was rewarded with slices of carrot.

Chapter Three

On Sunday afternoon, as Hetty returned home after taking Albert for a walk, she noticed nineteen year old Dee, sitting on the front doorstep of Hillside, the house next door where he lived. Dee whose name was Derek, a name he disliked, was the son of Margo Osborne who was the partner of Detective Inspector David Bray. The previous year, David had replaced Paul Fox after Paul had taken early retirement. Dee, who had failed his A-Levels dismally, was a wannabe musician and had started a band with three other like-minded people. To earn some money, he worked in the pasty shop.

As she always did, Hetty greeted the youngster and waved. To her surprise, Dee leapt to his feet and walked over to the wall between the two properties. "It might seem a silly question, but do you know the names of many puddings?"

Thinking she must have heard wrong, Hetty laughed.

"We need a name for our band, you see. The Jubilee committee have said we can play at the jubilee 'do' to get a bit of practice in but we don't have a name. I thought it'd be nice to have a pudding-like name. Sort of a tribute to Eddie. God rest his soul."

"But Eddie's band was Rhubarb Chutney," said Hetty, "So not a pudding."

"I know, but Ed told me they often referred to themselves as Rhubarb Crumble. Anyway, what do you think?"

"I think it's a good idea. When I was young, back in the sixties, one of my favourite bands, or groups as we called them back then, was Gooseberry Pie." Hetty sighed, "Such a long time ago. Anyway, I'm gasping for a cup of tea so why don't you come in and between you me and Lottie we'll see what we can come up with."

"Brill." To Hetty's amazement he leapt over the wall like an accomplished gymnast.

With mugs of tea, the sisters and Dee sat around the table in the living room. To aid their thinking, Lottie read out recipe titles from an old book she'd picked up at a jumble sale when first married. As well as puddings they looked at names of sweets. After an hour they had whittled a list of twenty down to four.

"So what's it to be? I think the decision must be yours, Dee."

Dee picked up his phone. "I'll text the names to the other band members and we'll go with the most popular." In a flash he'd sent out three messages. The four potential names were: Rum Butter, Peppermint Cream, Caramel Toffee and Treacle Toffee. To Lottie's delight, as it was her suggestion, Treacle Toffee was the favourite.

Thursday June the second saw the beginning of a four day celebration for The Queen's Platinum Jubilee and because Thursday and Friday were Bank Holidays, the charity shop closed after trade on Wednesday not to open again until the following Monday to allow the four ladies who ran it a well-deserved break.

Pentrillick's Jubilee committee had arranged to hold a street party on Friday June the third. However, at their first meeting they conceded it would be unreasonable to apply for the main street to be closed for the event. After consulting with James and Ella Dale, licensees of the Crown and Anchor, they opted instead to hold the party on the pub field.

Friday dawned a beautiful day with not a cloud in the Wedgewood blue sky and wall to wall sunshine. There was, however, a fresh wind blowing from the north which kept the temperature down in shaded areas.

The party was due to start at four o'clock. In the morning after several hours in the kitchen, Hetty and Lottie took their ease and watched a thanksgiving service for The Queen broadcast on television from St Pauls Cathedral. The Queen, however, due to discomfort from the previous day's celebrations, was not in attendance.

At half past three, the sisters walked down to the village with bulging bags of food. Hetty had made sandwiches, cheese straws and a quiche. Lottie, a selection of cakes and biscuits. On reaching the pub's field they made their way to a tent erected for food distribution where volunteers plated up the donations and placed them on the two lines of tables borrowed from the village hall and Pentrillick House.

The event was well attended with everyone who had the day free, whether patriotic or not, glad to mix and socialise with friends and neighbours. Hetty and Lottie sat with their friends, Debbie and her husband Gideon, and Kitty and her husband, Tommy. Opposite them sat retired Detective Inspector Paul Fox and much to the delight of many, newcomer, Layton Wolf. Paul eyed the glass in Hetty's hand. "Do my eyes deceive me or are you drinking something non-alcoholic?"

Hetty tutted. "Don't look so surprised. For what it's worth I seldom drink during the day unless it's a special occasion and although today is special I'm not drinking because Lottie and I will have a glass or two of wine at home tonight while we watch the party-cum-concert from the palace."

"Very wise."

"I shall be doing the same," said Layton, "although I might not drink as I'll be on my own. Having said that I'd be delighted if some of you would care to join me at home.

I've treated myself to a fifty-five inch TV and Clarence and George would enjoy the extra company."

"Fifty-five inches!" Lottie gasped, "Ours is only thirty-two."

Hetty nodded her head. "If you're serious we'd love to join you and we'll bring some wine."

"Please do. The more the merrier. How about you, Paul?"

"Yes, count me in."

"And you, ladies and gents?" He nodded in the direction of Debbie and Gideon and Kitty and Tommy.

"We'd be delighted," said Debbie.

The other three nodded their agreement.

Further down the field, Clara Bragg, the cook at the village care home, spotted Lottie's son Bill taking a seat at a table. "Ah, Billy," she gave him a hug, "I haven't seen you for ages. I see Sandra quite often at work and she tells me your entry for the Pentrillick in Bloom competition is to be in the newly created category, a vegetable plot."

He sat down. "That's right. I've dug up part of the lawn and so far it's going to plan. How about you?"

"I've done the same. Dug up part of my lawn, that is."

"Not doing tubs and hanging baskets then?"

"I'll do them but not enter them. How about you?"

"Sandra's doing ours and they will be entered. So why have you decided to enter the veg plot category?"

"To beat you of course." Clara patted his cheek and chuckling went off to join her friends.

"Well, I never," said Bill, "Cheeky moo."

"What was that about?" Sandra joined her husband with drinks bought in the pub.

"Clara is out to beat my veg plot in the Bloom competition."

"Ah, yes. She said something about that to me. She obviously likes you but at the same time has a bee in her bonnet about beating you. Remember how she went out of her way to beat your hanging baskets last time."

"Humph! How could I forget."

The next few weeks ran smoothly. Preparations for Zac and Emma's wedding gathered pace and invitations were sent out to family and friends. Villagers hoed, weeded, dead-headed and watered their gardens, tubs and baskets for the Pentrillick in Bloom Competition, and Lottie, Hetty and others were frequent visitors to Saltwater House. However, Layton declined reciprocating invitations and refused to say why. He also asked that everyone refrain from letting him know their addresses. Meanwhile, the Gardening Club met weekly and two weeks prior to the competition, they held their last meeting before the summer recess. Layton Wolf was guest speaker and the village hall was packed for the occasion.

On July the nineteenth, temperatures in some parts of England reached forty degrees centigrade, breaking all previous records. A few days later, schools broke up for the summer holiday and the tourist season was well underway. Campers arrived on the pub's field, guests booked into the Pentrillick Hotel and letting rooms of the Crown and Anchor, and all holiday cottages were occupied.

As July drew to a close and August dawned, villagers learned that the first half of the year had been the driest since 1911.

Inside the bathroom of the Old Bakehouse, the day before the Pentrillick in Bloom competition was to be judged, Bill knocked over a free-standing mirror while shaving. "Oh, for goodness sake," he cursed, "that means seven years' bad luck."

Sandra, collecting dirty washing from the linen basket on the landing, chuckled. "Now what have you done?"

"Broken a mirror. I really don't need any bad luck right now. Not with Clara hell bent on beating me with her veg plot."

"Oh dear, still never mind. I mean, Clara might have walked under a ladder, spilled salt, opened an umbrella indoors, crossed paths with a black cat or even seen a magpie."

"You're mocking me, Sandra."

"Yes dear. By the way, have you asked Tim who'll win?"

Bill slapped his forehead. "No. Silly me, I haven't time now so I'll do that when I get back from work."

After work, Bill placed lettuce leaves in two piles. Behind one he wrote his name, behind the other he wrote Clara. The twins, Vicki and Kate, home for the summer having finished their second year at university, watched as their father willed Tim in the direction of his name. To their amusement Tim headed for Clara's lettuce and happily tucked in to the lush green leaves.

That same day, Hetty and Lottie were working as per usual in the charity shop. The weather was glorious and they had the shop door open all morning to let in the fresh air and to welcome customers, most of whom were holiday makers. As they closed the shop for lunch, Lottie cast her eyes at the crystal ball shining in the glowing light of a lava lamp. "Last October, Het, you said that 2022 would be the best year ever and so far you've been spot on."

Hetty beamed. "Yes, I have to agree. The Jubilee weekend in particular was great fun and so was our seventieth birthday party in February, albeit a distant memory now. The drama group's production at Easter was a roaring success. We've had some beautiful warm, sunny weather and despite the lack of rain our garden is looking pretty good and ready for the Pentrillick in Bloom competition, especially our beach themed entry. What's more, we still have Zac and Emma's wedding to look forward to. Then of course there's Layton. His moving to the village has brought a bit of glamour to the place and that parrot of his is besotted with you as is Layton himself."

Much to her surprise, Lottie felt her face flush.

"And another thing," said Hetty, seeing her sister was lost for words, "we've managed to get over half way through the year without having a murder mystery to solve."

Lottie quickly found her voice. "Don't speak too soon, Het. Don't speak too soon."

Chapter Four

On Saturday, August the sixth, Hetty and Lottie woke and from their respective bedroom windows saw the front garden of Primrose Cottage was bathed in golden sunlight.

"I can't believe the weather's so favourable," said Hetty, excitedly over breakfast. "It'll make all the flowers look super nice today and our beach themed garden in particular should look impressive. I mean, it would have looked pretty sad had the judging been done in the pouring rain."

"Well, to be fair, the forecast said we were in for a long sunny spell of warm weather, possibly lasting as long as two weeks, so we must make the most of it. Having said that we really could do with some rain but not today. Definitely not today."

Round at the Old Bakehouse, Bill checked his vegetable plot only to find two of his lettuces had been part eaten by slugs or snails. To make matters worse, he spotted cabbage white caterpillars had nibbled at his brassicas. Hoping the damage wasn't too evident, he removed the damaged leaves from the cabbages and dug up the half eaten lettuce. In their place he planted parsley and basil from pots on the kitchen windowsill bought by Sandra the previous day. Praying she wouldn't notice they had gone before the judging took place, he moved around her houseplants to fill in the gaps.

There were three judges for the Pentrillick in Bloom Competition. Layton Wolf was asked by Tristan Liddicott-

Treen if he'd do the honours shortly after he had arrived in the village and that was the reason why he made a point of not knowing where anyone lived so that he would not be accused of being biased. The other judges were Claude Dexter, a cartoonist, known to Tristan and his family for many years but strangers to the inhabitants of the village, and Claude's wife, Member of Parliament, Simone Dexter.

The judging was due to take place from eleven o'clock onwards. Entrants had been issued with an approximate time and were asked either not to be at their properties or to stay indoors out of sight so their identity would remain unknown. Results were to be announced at seven o'clock on the Crown and Anchor field.

In the gardens of Saltwater House, Layton, relaxed in the shade of a cherry tree drinking coffee with George at his feet and Clarence chattering on a lower branch. He very much looked forward to the day. He'd already seen the displays of baskets and tubs along the main street and if they were anything to go by then the gardens should be equally impressive. At half past ten he went indoors to change and the animals went in with him. Before leaving, he stroked their heads and told them to behave.

Meanwhile, three hundred and seventy miles away, as Pentrillick's inhabitants plucked out last minute weeds and removed faded flowers from their displays, Shelley Sinclair was preparing to drive to Cornwall for a much anticipated holiday.

Shelley, an author of romantic, murder mystery fiction, lived in Canterbury in a modest detached house with her three cats and two dogs. She was in her late forties, had peroxide blonde hair and had never married or even had a serious relationship simply because no man lived up to the level of quality she accredited to her fictitious heart throbs. She had, however, had numerous affairs with married men but they meant nothing and she considered them to be justified as it was all part of her research.

Most of Shelley's works were based in her home town but on finishing her last creation she thought it would be nice to have a change. As she felt she had earned a holiday, she had decided to borrow a tent from her next door neighbours and spend a couple of weeks in Cornwall basing her next novel there.

Knowing very little of the county she had looked it up on-line and searched for a suitable campsite. To her delight she found that a pub called the Crown and Anchor situated in a village called Pentrillick, offered camping facilities on its field part laid to gardens. Campers were offered use of the pub's toilets - Ladies and Gents - both of which included a shower. Rather than just turn up she made a reservation for a plot and then to avoid being thought of as a Billy-no-mates, she rang her cousin Beatrice to see if she would like a holiday in Cornwall too. Beatrice had eagerly agreed. She was married to Brian, a man who spent all of his spare time fishing or playing golf and who thought holidays were an unnecessary expense. Therefore, Brian was happy to hear that his wife intended to go away for a couple of weeks; for not only would he be able to fish and play golf without her nagging but he'd also be able to smoke in the house, pop to the pub each night and eat what his wife considered to be unhealthy food. To make sure he was able to enjoy his freedom to its full extent, he booked the two weeks off work.

Before she set off on her journey, Shelley took her two dogs to the kennels where she had arranged board for two weeks. The cats she left in the care of her neighbours. There was a cat flap on the back door of her house and so the felines had twenty-four seven access. She gave her neighbours a key so they could keep an eye on the animals, feed them and make sure they had water to drink.

Shelley left her home shortly after lunch in her cream coloured Morris Traveller; a car she had inherited from her father who had owned it from new. It was immaculate and her pride and joy. En route to the West Country she picked up her cousin Beatrice, who being a school dinner lady was footloose and fancy free for the duration of the school's summer holiday. Shelley knew that her cousin was quiet, kept herself to herself and read a lot, so would not interrupt her thoughts if and when ideas for her new book began to flow.

The cousins arrived in Pentrillick at seven o'clock that evening to find a large gathering of people on the edge of the pub's field near to the car park. Unaware as to who they might be, Shelley told Beatrice to wait in the car. She then went into the pub to announce their arrival where landlady, Ella Dale, greeted her and took her outside to view the door leading into the toilets for use of both pub clientele and campers. While there, intrigued, Shelley nodded towards the crowd of people and asked the reason for the gathering.

Ella looked at her watch. "They'll be in soon after the judges have finished announcing the winners. It's the Pentrillick in Bloom Competition, you see. It's a very popular event and nearly everyone enters in one category or another."

"Ah, that'll explain the abundance of colourful hanging baskets and tubs of flowers along the main street. I commented on it to Beat. We were both very impressed."

"Yes, the locals have done the village proud again."

"Is it an annual event then?"

"It will be but this is only the second. It was knocked on the head for the last two years for obvious reasons."

Shelley groaned. "Covid."

Ella nodded as she opened a door between the toilets and the pub. "This door is of course locked when the pub's closed but the outside door is always left unlocked when

27

there are campers on the field." As Ella pushed the door open, Shelley saw they were back in the public bar.

"Brilliant. So where shall we pitch our tent?"

"Anywhere you like on the left hand side of the field overlooking the gardens. There are plenty of spaces because being Saturday several people went home today."

After wishing the cousins a good holiday, Ella returned behind the bar and Shelley joined Beatrice outside where the presentations were still in progress with intermittent peals of laughter and rounds of applause.

After driving slowly across the field, the ladies selected a plot beside a caravan reasoning that it together with the tall hedge running along the back of the field would provide shade and help keep the tent cool in the hot weather. Aware the light would be fading by nine o'clock, they quickly erected their temporary home while visibility was still good. Feeling pleased with their efforts they went into the pub, bought drinks and ordered something to eat. By then the competition results and presentation had long concluded and the majority of the gathering had moved indoors. Drawn by the jubilant atmosphere, the cousins were thrilled to join in with the celebrations. When Shelley went to the bar for drinks, landlady Ella asked if everything was okay. Shelley told her that they had pitched their tent beside a caravan.

"Lovely," said Ella, "that's our caravan and Harry, the son of me and him over there," she nodded towards her husband, James, "is staying in it having just finished his last year at university. Currently he's alone but on Monday he'll be joined by two fellow students. Needless to say, if there's any bother you must let us know."

Shelley was delighted. With the occupants of the caravan being the son of the licensees, it was unlikely he and his friends would make a lot of noise and disturb her train of thought while thinking up a plot for her first Cornish novel.

Shelley watched the pub's clientele with interest, hoping to fire up her imagination and spot a dashingly handsome man on whose looks to base her villain. She was not disappointed. Several men filled the criterion, likewise a few women seemed suitable for her damsel in distress. She was particularly taken by the banter between a man and woman who appeared to have been in rivalry over a category in the Pentrillick in Bloom competition. It was obvious the female had won first place and the male third. The woman addressed the man as Bill and he addressed her as Clara. Shelley chuckled. Perhaps she'd have a flower competition in her book. She knew absolutely nothing about horticulture but with the aid of the internet she was willing to learn the basics.

Over by the fireplace, Hetty and Lottie having won first prize for their seaside themed garden, were celebrating with their friends. Bernie the boatman who had loaned them a lobster pot, having heard of their win, congratulated them.

"I can't believe we even got a prize," chuckled Hetty, "Let alone it being first. Just shows there's no accounting for taste."

"I think it was because we threw in a bit of humour and you must admit the plastic lobster we bought in the charity shop had a certain amount of charm."

Bernie tutted. "I don't know how you got away with that lobster. I mean, it was the wrong colour for a start."

"Wrong colour?" Hetty was confused.

Kitty slapped her hand across her mouth. "Oh, yes it was, Het. Lobsters are blue. It's the cooking that turns them red."

"So we had a cooked lobster in our pot," gasped Hetty, "well, I never."

"That's probably why you won," chuckled Bernie.

"Most likely," agreed Lottie, "Anyway, it was fun to do and the judges clearly appreciated our efforts."

"Especially the MP's husband, Claude or whatever he's called," remarked Hetty. "He seemed a real good sport when dishing out the prizes and his jokes were actually funny."

Claude Dexter had good reason to feel jubilant. He and his wife, Simone, worked hard and had little free time. Hence when Tristan Liddicott-Treen had asked them to take part in the judging they had eagerly accepted. Initially they had planned to stay at Pentrillick House for the weekend as guests of Tristan and his wife Samantha, but after mulling it over they decided to make a proper holiday of it and stay for three whole weeks. Because their up-country home was in a remote rural area; they thanked the Liddicott-Treens for their kind offer of accommodation but said after reading about Pentrillick on the internet they had decided to rent The Old Lifeboat House and enjoy its fantastic view of the open sea. Claude, a freelance cartoonist, loved his chosen career and anticipated the change of scenery might be an inspiration for his work. His wife, Simone, an MP since 2019, had before then been a general practitioner but when the opportunity arose for a change of career, she had jumped at the chance. As for the holiday in Cornwall, she intended to put it to good use and keep in touch with her constituents on-line.

The following morning, Hetty and Lottie prepared to go to church. Donned in their best dresses, glad of the warm weather for a suitable chance to wear them, they walked down Long Lane and into the village. As they approached the church for the service at nine, Hetty nodded towards two women on the opposite side of the road. "I recognise them. They were in the pub last night and the blonde one wearing the pink shorts was ogling all the men. I reckon she's one to watch."

Lottie laughed. "Well, we've nothing to worry about, have we? I mean, neither of us have a partner so no-one for her to nobble if that's what her intentions are."

Shelley and Beatrice, not having slept too well under canvas, were making their way through the village for breakfast at Taffeta's Tea Shoppe unaware they were being scrutinised. According to a leaflet they had picked up inside the pub, the tea shoppe opened at nine and both ladies were gasping for a cup of tea. Happy the morning was again bright and sunny and cheered by the church bells ringing, both looked forward to an enjoyable holiday.

"I think we ought to buy a little gas thing and a camping kettle," said Beatrice, as the waitress placed a tea tray on their table, "I don't mind waiting for something to eat in the morning but I do like a cup of tea when I first wake up."

Shelley broke her croissant in half. "I couldn't agree more. We'll have a wander round the village later and see if anywhere sells that sort of thing."

After breakfast they ambled back to the campsite where they took a walk around the field to look at the gardens and get an idea of how many campers there were. In all they counted six tents, two motor homes, three caravans other than the static one beside their tent, and one camper van. The camper van was on the far end of the field and its owner, a young man in his early thirties, sat outside on the grass quietly strumming a guitar.

After they arrived home from church, Lottie and Hetty began to prepare lunch for Debbie and her husband Gideon, Kitty and her husband Tommy, Layton Wolf and Paul Fox. In Layton's case it was to return his hospitality. Paul was invited along to make up the numbers and because he and Layton had become good friends. Usually the sisters went to the Crown and Anchor on Sunday for a roast dinner but the warm weather had curtailed that routine: instead they chose to stay at home and have something less filling.

The guests were invited to arrive any time after midday ready to eat at one-thirty so that Kitty had ample time between lunch and playing the organ at Evensong. To their surprise the first to appear was Layton. Not sure how long the walk would take he had left Saltwater House at eleven-thirty to make sure he was in good time. When he reached the gates and realised that Primrose Cottage was the house with the beach themed garden, he began to chuckle.

"I might have known this would be where you two lived." He kissed the cheeks of each sister in turn as they went out to meet him: "A cooked lobster in a crab pot indeed."

"Oh dear, we hoped no-one would notice," confessed Lottie. "Well, actually that's not quite true because neither of us realised lobsters are blue until Bernie the boatman pointed it out in the pub last night. We borrowed the crab pot from him, you see."

"I'll let you into a little secret. Neither Claude nor I twigged it either. We both agreed the garden, your garden, was wonderful. It was Simone who pointed out the colour was wrong but Claude and I didn't care. As far as we were concerned it was the best themed garden we'd seen." He shook his head. "Can't believe it was you two though."

Just after five, Shelley and Beatrice, tired, happy and slightly sunburnt, returned from the beach with a small camping stove, a kettle, two mugs, two plastic plates and a pack of cheap metal cutlery purchased from the beach shop. When they walked onto the camping field they found a large, colourful wigwam had appeared beside their tent. Parked alongside it was a silver estate car but there was no sign of its owners. This was because the four females who had hired the wigwam were inside the Crown and Anchor celebrating the beginning of their holiday with glasses of sparkling wine.

The four girls were friends who had met at their local gym where one of them, Gretel, was a fitness instructor. Aged between twenty and twenty-five, they had lots of energy and intended to cram as much as they could into their two week stay.

"Oh to be young again," said Kitty, wistfully, dropping off a poster advertising the church's summer fete en route to play the organ at Evensong.

Tess agreed. "Yes, and it'll be interesting to see if they are as boisterous at the end of their holiday as they are now."

"I doubt they will be. Not once the old sea air gets to them."

"True, being townies they'll not be used to it."

"So out of interest, where are they from?"

"Reading, apparently, and they're all fitness enthusiasts."

Chapter Five

At six o'clock on Monday morning, Shelley woke, popped on her dressing gown and walked across the field to the Ladies. The sun was already shining brightly, there was not a cloud in the cornflower-blue sky and the only sound was that of bird song. Not expecting to see anyone on her way back to the tent, she was surprised to find the four girls outside their wigwam dressed in shorts and tee shirts doing exercises.

"Good heavens! Bit early for PE, isn't it, girls?"

Gretel, the fitness instructor, smiled sweetly. "Not at all. We need to warm up before we go for our run. Got to go early as it'll be too hot later."

"A run! Where to?"

"Along the coastal path and back today. We won't go too far though. Eight miles at the most."

"Eight miles! Rather you than me."

Inside their tent, Beatrice was up and straightening her sleeping bag. While she went for a shower, Shelley got dressed and then lit the gas stove. As the water came to the boil, the girls waved and said they were off. Shelley watched as they slipped through a gap in the hedge and onto the cliff path.

"Mad," she whispered, "stark staring mad." Then she caught sight of the roll of fat hanging over the top of her shorts. "On the other hand, a bit of exercise might be a good thing. I'll suggest it to Beat when she gets back."

On her return, Beatrice scowled at the idea. "It's going to be far too hot to exercise, Shell, so I suggest we just take the occasional dip in the sea instead. After all we are on holiday."

Shelley agreed and as the weather was glorious they decided to spend the entire day on the beach and when they were hungry, one of them would pop along to the pasty shop to purchase something for their lunch.

Later that same day, having swapped days working in the charity shop with Daisy and Maisie, Hetty and Lottie sat side by side on a bench in the sunshine on Penzance station's platform one waiting for the 15.07 train due in from London Paddington. Lottie was apprehensive; on the train were her daughter, Barbara who she had not seen for seven years and with Barbara, Jed her partner of two years, who Lottie had never met.

Barbara lived and worked in the United States and had done so for twenty-five years. Originally she went over there to work with the advertising firm with whom she had been employed since leaving school. After that her career progressed, she learned to love the country and eventually became a citizen. Although she'd had several relationships which had lasted for a number of years, she always let it be known she had no maternal instincts thus no desire to settle down and raise a family. Barbara Burton, a woman in her mid to late forties was independent, strong minded and strong willed. Quite the opposite to her widowed mother, Lottie.

The sisters stood up as the train pulled into the station on time and watched the doors as people stepped from the carriages onto the platform and made their way to the exit.

Barbara and Jed were the last to appear; their exit hampered by the large amount of luggage they shared. When Lottie saw them she frantically waved and then ran into the outstretched arms of her daughter.

"Mum, you're looking really well."

"Thank you, and so are you."

"Auntie Het," Hetty received a hug too, "it's lovely to see you." She turned to the man who stood amongst the luggage, "And this is Jed, Jed Hanks". She took his arm and pulled him forwards."

"Pleased to meet you, ma'am." He shook Lottie's hand and then turned to Hetty, "and you too, ma'am."

"Hanks," said Lottie, "Any relation to Tom?"

"Not that I know, ma'am."

Jed was over six feet tall, he had blue eyes, sandy coloured hair tinged with grey and an engaging smile. Lottie and Hetty liked him instantly.

"How's my darling brother?" Barbara asked, "I can't wait to see him and his family. The Old Bakehouse too. It sounds wonderful."

"Much the same," said Lottie, "Looking forward to seeing you and meeting Jed too."

"How many children do Bill and his wife have?" Jed asked.

"Three," replied Lottie, "Zac whose wedding you're here for, and twins, Vicki and Kate."

"Then there's Crumpet the dog and Jim, a newly acquired tortoise," Hetty added.

Barbara shook her head, "Oh yes, I've heard all about the tortoise and seen pictures of him too. According to Bill the animal is psychic."

"So he likes to believe," said Lottie. "Having said that, we have a crystal ball in the charity shop where we work part-time and like to consult it now and again."

"A crystal ball and a psychic tortoise," chuckled Jed, "I think I'm gonna enjoy my vacation here."

Because they had three spare bedrooms, two due to a loft conversation, it had been agreed that Barbara and Jed would stay with Lottie and Hetty at Primrose Cottage for the duration of their visit. They were allotted the double room in the loft extension with panoramic views of the sea to the front and a picturesque landscape to the back.

In the evening after they had settled in and had something to eat, Barbara and Jed were taken down to the village and along the main street to the Old Bakehouse where Barbara's brother Bill lived with his wife Sandra and two teenage twin daughters, Kate and Vicki.

It was a heart-warming reunion. The siblings had not seen each other for almost seven years and no-one had before met Jed. Like Lottie and Hetty, Sandra and Bill liked him instantly.

"Now before anything else is said, Jed and I have something to tell you." Barbara pulled her left hand from the pocket of her jacket held it up for all to see, "I'm delighted to say that Jed and I are married. We had a small, no fuss ceremony back home for just a group of close friends and now we're here we would like to take you all out at some point for a meal to celebrate."

Bill kissed his sister's cheek and slapped Jed on the back. "Well done, mate. Barbara here always insisted she'd never get wed so that's quite an achievement on your part."

Jed glowed. "She didn't take much persuading."

Lottie hugged her daughter and new son-in-law. "I'm absolutely thrilled to bits, I really am. This news has made my day," she stepped back. "So how long have you been married?"

"Just over two weeks," said Barbara, "on July the twenty-third."

After the wedding talk, Sandra made tea for everyone and they all sat out in the back garden.

"What do you think of Cornwall?" Sandra asked, "What little you've seen, that is."

"It's very pretty," enthused Barbara, "and I loved the castle on the island. Saint Michaels Mount I think Auntie Het said it's called. And this village of yours is so colourful. I've never seen so many flowers."

37

"Ah, that's because we have a competition called Pentrillick in Bloom. The first was in 2019 but because of the Covid thing this is only the second and it's really taken off. Everyone seems to have had a go. Hence all the flowers."

"And people had plenty of time on their hands to make plans during the lockdowns," added Hetty.

Barbara groaned at the mention of lockdowns.

"So when is it judged," Jed asked, "this flower competition?"

"It already has been. Judging was last Saturday and we won best themed garden this year." Hetty spoke with pride.

"And our hanging baskets and tubs came second in their category," said Sandra.

"And my vegetable plot came third." Bill recalled the look of glee on Clara's face and scowled.

"You are a green fingered bunch," laughed Barbara. "My horticultural skills are zilch."

"So what line of work are you in, Jed?" Sandra asked. "I don't think we've ever been told that."

Jed smiled broadly. "I'm a cop with New York Police."

Both Hetty and Lottie's jaws dropped.

Bill chuckled. "You'll have a couple of admirers with Mum and Auntie Het then. They're great fans of solving any crimes that happen in the village."

"Well if anything should occur during the next few weeks, remember ladies, I'm on vacation."

Later in the evening, Bill and Sandra took Barbara and Jed to the Crown and Anchor for a drink. Hetty and Lottie, although asked, said they would not join them as they wanted the siblings and their partners to spend some time together.

Cousins Shelley and Beatrice, sunburnt from their day on the beach, were already in the pub having popped in for a bite to eat only to discover it was quiz night. However, they agreed that to do the quiz might be fun and so sat in a corner by a piano. As they sipped their drinks, Shelley, a people-watcher, was able to observe the clientele and their mannerisms. When Bill and the family arrived, Shelley pleased to observe people of a similar age to Beatrice and herself, watched as the two ladies sat down at a table. "You sit down too, Bill, I'll get the drinks," she heard the taller of the two men say.

Shelley's jaw dropped. "That handsome brute's an American, Beat. Ideal, I'll focus on him and maybe make him the hero in my new book. Or perhaps even the villain."

Beatrice followed the direction of her cousin's eyes. "Yes, he is rather gorgeous, I must admit. Do you think he lives around here?"

"I don't know. We'll keep an eye on him and the people he's with and try to find out."

Fifteen minutes before the quiz was due to begin, the young man they had seen outside the camper van arrived. After buying a pint of cider he looked around the bar.

"Poor lad looks lonely. Do you think he's looking for somewhere to sit?" Shelley asked Beatrice.

"Probably. I expect he'd like to sit on a proper seat after sitting on the grass and there can't be a lot of room in his camper van."

On hearing Beatrice's response, Shelley beckoned the young man over. "There's a seat here if you don't mind being in the company of two middle-aged ladies."

His smile stretched from ear to ear. "I'd be delighted to sit with you if you don't mind."

"We don't mind at all and you can help us with the quiz."

"Thank you, I like quizzes although I'm not very good at them." He sat down. "It's nice to have someone to talk to. I've been here since Saturday but I don't know anyone yet."

39

"Same with us. My name is Shelley by the way, and this is my cousin, Beatrice."

"Pleased to meet you." They were surprised to see him hesitate: "My name is err Happy, Happy Harper."

"Happy?" Shelley wondered if she had heard correctly.

"Yes, I'm afraid so."

"Is that your proper name or a nickname?" Beatrice was equally surprised.

The young man blushed. "My real name, would you believe. Apparently I was born smiling. This is according to my mother who I might add was then and still is at times away with the fairies and so I think the combination of gas and air during labour might have had some impact on her observation. I'm used to it now of course but I always find it embarrassing when I need to introduce myself to anyone. Of course, I could change my name by deed poll but that would upset Mum and I wouldn't want to do that."

Shelley patted the back of his hand. "No, leave it as it is. I think it's rather charming especially if you live up to it."

"I try."

"So are you here alone?" Beatrice assumed he was because he said 'I' and not 'we' have been here since Saturday, however she wanted confirmation.

"Yes, and I intend to do a bit of surfing and take some photos while I'm here. I'm a photographer, you see, and I like the idea of taking pictures of the Cornish coastline and landscapes too."

Beatrice was surprised. Happy bore no resemblance at all to the image conjured up in her mind of a surfer. His hair was short and neatly trimmed, he was slightly overweight and his skin was pale.

"So what do you photograph when at home?" Shelley, who liked taking pictures herself, was interested.

"Weddings, christenings, funerals. You name it and I'll be there."

"Funerals?" Beatrice was taken aback.

"Yes, it's not something I do on a regular basis but some people like to have a record of the day as family members are understandably often too preoccupied to see who is present and so forth. Needless to say, my presence is subtle and I use a telescopic lens to enable me to keep my distance."

"Very interesting." Ice cubes rattled as Shelley took a sip of her gin and tonic. "So how long are you here for?"

Happy shrugged his shoulders. "Not sure. My time's my own and I've purposely not taken on any jobs throughout August."

"But surely August is a popular month for weddings," reasoned Beatrice.

"It is, yes, but there's no shortage of photographers back home and if I'm honest it's not my favourite type of gig. Too much hanging around waiting to capture the significant moments of the ceremony and reception. Anyway, I wanted to take a break now because during term times I take evening classes twice a week so holidays have to fit in with that."

"Evening classes. As a tutor?" Beatrice asked.

"Yes."

Shelley nodded approvingly. "And your subject I assume is photography."

"Well, not quite right. In fact not right at all. I teach knitting."

"Knitting!" Beatrice was flabbergasted, "I didn't realise men did knitting."

"Oh but they do. In fact most of my pupils are men."

Chapter Six

On Tuesday morning, having swapped their Monday/Tuesday shifts with Maisie and Daisy to enable them to meet Barbara and Jed at the railway station, Hetty and Lottie, trundled off down the hill to the charity shop wearing the thin summery dresses they had worn to church on Sunday. The morning trade was fairly brisk and most of the customers were holiday makers browsing, glad to get indoors out of the blazing sun. During a lull when they were alone in the shop, Lottie asked Hetty if the crystal ball, which had been neglected for a while, had anything to say. "Let's have a look." With a chuckle Hetty cast her hands over the glass orb. "Oh," she muttered wistfully, "I see a garden. A cottage garden and very beautiful it is too."

Lottie sighed. "Wishful thinking there then. I'd like to be in a cottage garden right now sitting in the shade of a weeping willow with a glass of ice-cold cranberry juice."

As her words faded, the shop door opened and in walked cartoonist, Claude Dexter who with his MP wife had judged the entries for the Pentrillick in Bloom competition.

"Good morning, ladies. It's a shot in the dark, I know, but I wonder if you have any pieces of Aynsley china. I collect it you see and I'm particularly interested in extending my Cottage Garden collection."

Utterly astonished, Lottie's jaw dropped while Hetty cast a look of awe at the crystal ball.

"Actually, I think we do," said Lottie, finding her voice. "They're in the cabinet over here." She led Claude to the glass fronted display case beneath the counter. Taking a key from a jar by the till she unlocked the door and took out a small vase and a pin dish.

"Excellent." Claude took the pin dish from Lottie and examined it; he then stood it on the counter and looked at the vase. "I don't have either of these so I'll take them both."

"Thank you. They are very pretty. Don't you think so, Het?"

"What? Oh, yes. Yes. Very pretty." Hetty forced a smile. "Lovely weather," she said, eager to talk about anything other than cottage gardens.

"Certainly is and the heat along with the sea air is doing Simone and me the world of good."

"Oh, yes, nothing like it although it's a touch too hot for me." Avoiding her sister's eyes, Lottie carefully wrapped the two china items.

Claude took a debit card from his wallet and swiped it over the machine. "Would I be right in thinking you two ladies won a prize in the gardening competition? I'm sure I presented you with a cheque but can't remember the category."

Lottie placed the wrapped goods in a brown paper bag. "You're right. We won first prize and it embarrasses me to admit that it was for our themed garden."

Claude roared with laughter. "Ah, yes. The cooked lobster in a crab pot. Made my day that even though I didn't spot the error 'til Simone pointed it out."

After bidding the ladies farewell he left the shop with his purchases, still laughing. As the door closed, Hetty looked at Lottie. "That ball's starting to freak me out."

"Coincidence," said Lottie.

"Maybe, but the timing was uncanny."

"Yes, I'll grant you that but there's no way that ball can predict things and the same goes for Bill and his so-called psychic tortoise."

In the evening, Hetty, Lottie, Kitty and Debbie met up at the Crown and Anchor to put the world to rights. They were not surprised to find their favourite table near to the fireplace was taken but weren't too concerned as being summer no fire was lit and in the hearth stood a large jug of dried flowers and grasses. Because the bar was busy they sat at the only table vacant by the open French doors leading onto the sun terrace overlooking the beach. Shortly after they had bought drinks, Jed and Barbara arrived back from a visit to Marazion and spoke briefly to the ladies. They then joined Bill and Sandra at the bar who led them into the dining room where they had a table booked for dinner. Shelley, seated on the next table with Beatrice, heard what was said and had to know more.

"Excuse me, but do you know that handsome American gentleman?" She tilted back her chair to address the ladies.

Lottie beamed with pride. "Yes, he's my son-in-law and his name is Jed; the young woman with him is my daughter, Barbara. They're here for the wedding of my grandson early next month." She nodded towards the bar, "That's Zac, my grandson over there wearing the striped shirt and with him is his fiancée, Emma."

"Good looking family you have. So what line of work is the American gentleman in? I ask because he looks quite authoritative."

"He's a police officer."

Shelley clapped her hands with glee. "I knew it. I'm sure he won't mind but I'm going to use his looks to describe the hero in my next book."

"You're a writer?" It was Hetty who spoke.

"Yes, I write murder mystery books with a good dollop of romance and it's time I had a character from across the pond."

"May I ask your name?" Debbie already had her phone open ready to Google the answer.

"Shelley Sinclair." Shelley proffered her hand, "And this lady with me is my cousin, Beatrice."

"And are you a writer too, Beatrice?" Kitty asked.

Beatrice blushed. "Good heavens, no. I love to read but lack the imagination needed to write even a short story let alone a book. I don't know how Shell does it."

"I take it you're down here on holiday then?" Lottie commented.

"Yes, and close by. We're camping in the pub gardens here."

Debbie looked up from her phone. "Ideal if you like a drink in the evening."

Shelley nodded. "That's just what I thought. Convenient for the shops and beach as well."

"So, will the murder in your new book take place on a campsite?" Lottie asked.

Shelley shook her head. "No, no, on the beach. I'm thinking along the lines of a beach party but it's early days yet."

Kitty noticed Hetty had gone very quiet, was frowning and looked paler than usual. "Are you alright, Het?"

"Yes, yes, I'm fine. Well no, I'm a bit shocked. It's daft I know but you see, last October I plucked a name out of the air for an author and that name was Shelley Sinclair."

Debbie's jaw dropped. "Yes, of course. I thought the name sounded familiar. I was in the shop with you at the time and you said you saw it in the crystal ball thing. That's freaky."

Shelley laughed. "You must have seen my name somewhere and it registered without you realising."

"Maybe," Hetty wasn't convinced.

"You mentioned the title of a book too, Het. What was it?"

Hetty looked even more embarrassed. "If you remember I said the name was inspired by the tide table on the charity shop wall and it was called *High Jinks at High Tide*."

45

"What!" gasped Shelley, "But that is the title of my next book. There's no way you could have known that because I only thought of it the other day and I've told no-one. Not even Beatrice."

"I think I need another glass of wine," whimpered Hetty. "Anyone care to join me?"

All said yes.

"Please, please, allow me to get them," gushed Shelley, leaping to her feet and taking her purse from her handbag, "And then you can tell me all about this crystal ball."

When they all had drinks, Hetty and Lottie explained how the previous summer, Maisie and Daisy were working in the charity shop when they received a delivery of items from a shop that had ceased trading. Amongst the goods were fishermen's colourful glass balls and because one, made of clear glass, was without its lattice string work and they thought it unsellable, they put it on the counter and for a laugh pretended it was a crystal ball.

Shelley was fascinated and vowed she'd pop in the shop sometime and see it for herself. Meanwhile, Beatrice recognising a few faces, asked who certain people were. "And why do I know that lady sitting by the piano with her chap?" she asked.

Debbie looked over her shoulder. "Oh, that's Dolly and with her is her partner, Sid. Dolly runs the pasty shop with her friend, Eve."

"Of course, that's where I've seen her."

"And what does Sid do?" Shelley asked.

"He's a plumber but when we first met him he told fortunes." Hetty chuckled: "He called himself Psychic Sid."

"Really!" Shelley gazed at Sid in awe. "He sounds like someone we need to meet. But that's for another day."

At half past ten, Shelley and Beatrice thanked the ladies for their company and said goodnight. As they approached the exit, they saw Happy Harper chatting with the licensees' son, Harry. Glad to see he was making friends, they wished him goodnight and he nodded in response.

Hetty, having recovered from shock, watched as they left the building and then turned to Debbie. "I saw you Google her. What did you find out?"

"She's written seventeen books and they seem to sell reasonably well. I've already bought one for my Kindle so I'll let you know what I think when I've read it."

"Brilliant. When we get in I'll see if she's on Facebook and if she is I'll send her a friend request. It'll be nice to follow her progress."

"And in the morning we'll look to see if there are any of her books in the charity shop," said Lottie, "because I'd feel a lot happier if there was a chance you'd seen her name there."

"So would I," agreed Hetty, "but that still wouldn't explain the crystal ball foretelling the name of a book yet to be written."

Chapter Seven

The following morning, Hetty and Lottie were working in the charity shop with the door wide open to let in the breeze when Clara Bragg stepped excitedly over the threshold. She quickly glanced around the shop. "Have you any books by … umm …" she took a piece of paper from her pocket, "Shelley Sinclair?"

The sisters were both surprised.

"Without looking we can actually say no to that," said Hetty, "simply because we met her last night and so went through the bookcase with a fine toothcomb this morning to see if we had any of her work."

Clara's shoulders slumped. "Damn! It's not often we have a famous author in the village and I want a copy of anything she wrote so I can get her to sign it. I've looked on-line and ordered her most recent book which came out in January but a cook's pay doesn't allow for too many luxuries so I can only afford the one."

"I don't want to downplay her achievements but Shelley's hardly a *famous* author," said Hetty.

"Maybe not but she might be one day. You never know."

"True, I suppose."

"But if you've ordered one of her books on-line surely she can sign that," reasoned Lottie.

"Yes, I know, but I want to give the impression that I'm a great fan and have lots of her books even though I'd never heard of her 'til yesterday when I bumped into Tess in the pasty shop and she told me about her."

Lottie smothered a smile. "Well she and a cousin are camping on the pub field and are likely to be here for a fortnight, so if someone does drop a copy or two in we'll let you know."

"Bless you," Clara gave Lottie a hug. "Must dash or I'll be late for work."

That same day, Shelley set off for the beach and en route bought a pasty from Great Aunt Esme's Pasty Shop. While there, Sid and Zac arrived to buy pasties for their lunch.

"I recognise you," gushed Shelley. "You were in the pub last night and my new friends told me of your erstwhile occupation." She held out her hand: "delighted to meet you Psychic Sid."

Sid laughed. "Blimey. It's a few years since I did that."

"Were you any good?"

"No, I was rubbish and made it up as I went along. It were a bit of fun though. I'm back into plumbing now. It's a bit more reliable."

Shelley turned to Zac. "And would I be right in thinking you're the young man soon to be wed?"

"Yes, that's right. Just over three weeks to go now."

"How exciting. Well, I wish you well."

"Thank you."

"You're welcome." Shelley took her pasty from the counter, left the shop and walked the short distance along the main street to an alleyway that led down to the beach. As anticipated the beach was busy. Having overindulged in the sun a few days earlier, she opted to sit against a wall where there was a little shade. Once comfortable she ate her pasty and then took her notepad and pen from her bag. Beneath the heading, *High Jinks at High Tide,* she began to outline a plot.

Beatrice, meanwhile, to allow Shelley time to herself, had taken the bus into Penzance to have a look around and to buy a few groceries. She said she'd have lunch in town and hoped to be back in Pentrillick around five o'clock.

Just before five, Shelley left the beach and called in at the shop for sun cream. The bottle she had brought with her was getting low and she hoped once the weather cooled a little to spend more days in the sun. While in the shop she spotted a stack of disposable barbecues. The previous evening, campers at the far end of the field had had a barbecue outside their tent; the idea appealed to her and so she added one to her basket, thinking it would be nice to dine al fresco one evening and save a few pennies too. However, when she went to pay for her goods she was surprised to be asked by the shop assistant where she proposed to use the barbecue as they wouldn't sell to people intending to take them out into the countryside because of the risk of fire. Shelley was pleased to hear the caution and assured the shop keeper the barbecue would be used safely on the campsite and would not be out of her sight.

Later that afternoon, Jake and Jack, friends of the licensees' son Harry, arrived. As neither drove they had travelled down by train and Landlady Ella took Harry to the station in Penzance to meet them. Shelley was taking a shower when they arrived at the campsite; Beatrice, back from her shopping trip, was sitting outside the tent reading. Working as a dinner lady at a secondary school she was used to young people and so greeted them warmly and said she hoped they enjoyed their stay.

In the evening as Bill and Sandra's twin daughters, Vicki and Kate, arrived at the Crown and Anchor for an evening's waitressing, they saw Harry and his two friends sitting at one of the picnic benches on the pub field. Harry beckoned them over.

"Girls come and meet my mates, Jake and Jack." He pointed to the two lads with him. Jake was tall, dark-haired and bespectacled; Jack was very slim and wore his long blond hair in a bun.

Jake jumped up. "Hey, great to meet you. I take it you live here."

"We do," said Vicki, "at the Old Bakehouse."

"If you're going in the pub for a drink, why don't we join you?" Jack was already on his feet.

"That would be nice," said Kate, "but we have to work first."

"Oh. You work in Harry's pub then?"

"Yes, but only during the holidays when we're home from uni," said Vicki.

"Cool. So you're both at uni." Jack sat back down. "We were but we've all finished now and so need to find worthwhile jobs."

"Good luck with that," said Kate. "Anyway, we must go or we'll be late and I expect it'll be busy tonight because Treacle Toffee are playing."

"Yeah," said Harry, "Dad mentioned that so we'll be in to see them later, and when you've finished work we'd love you to join us and tell us what you hope to do in the future."

"Great, we look forward to it." Vicki's eyes shone as they dashed towards the entrance to the pub.

Treacle Toffee had played there every other Wednesday since James, impressed by their first performance at the Platinum Jubilee celebrations, had offered them the chance to play for a modest fee. Two of the band members lived in Pentrillick; nineteen year old Dee Osborne, next door neighbour to Hetty and Lottie, and Lewis Peters, who worked in the village garage as a mechanic. The other two were lads from Penzance who had applied to join Dee and Lewis after seeing their advert on social media about forming a band.

Shelley and Beatrice, liking the idea of musical entertainment, went in for a drink and something to eat just after nine and found the place packed. The band had stopped for a twenty minute break and drinkers were eagerly refilling their glasses before the second half began.

As the cousins waited at the bar for a table after buying drinks and ordering food, they saw an elderly couple get up to leave in a dimly lit corner near to the piano. Eager to sit down, they quickly grabbed the vacated table where much to Shelley's delight, she spotted an electricity socket nearby. Knowing her phone battery was low, she plugged in her charger and then looked to see if she had any emails. When she checked Facebook she smiled.

"I've a friend request from one of the ladies we met last night."

"Is it the one whose daughter is married to the American?"

"No, it's Hetty, her sister." Shelley granted the request.

After they had eaten, both had another drink but Beatrice was unable to finish hers. She said she had a touch of indigestion, was extremely tired and needed to lie down. Not wanting to keep her cousin up, Shelley quickly finished her drink. On leaving the pub they popped into the Ladies, cleaned their teeth and then wandered back to their tent where Beatrice promptly sat down on her camp bed and removed her shoes.

Shelley placed her handbag by her suitcase. "You'll probably think me mad, Bee, but I'm going to take a stroll down to the beach. It's a lovely clear night, the moon is almost full and I rather like the idea of sitting on one of the benches and watching the sea for a while. You don't mind, do you?"

Beatrice took her pyjamas from beneath her pillow and unfolded them. "Of course not and I don't think you're mad at all. In fact I'd offer to go with you but I did rather a lot of walking today in Penzance and no doubt that along with the excessive heat is why I'm feeling tired, my muscles ache, and I feel hot and shivery. I'm sure if I can get a good night's sleep then I'll feel as right as rain in the morning."

"I hope you do because the forecast is for another scorcher tomorrow so we must go for a dip in the sea,"

Shelley looked through her luggage for her favourite cardigan.

"I'd take a blanket as well if I were you then you can put it over your legs. It might be quite chilly just sitting now the sun's gone down and there's nearly always a breeze by the sea."

"Good idea," Shelley took the blanket she had covering her sleeping bag and neatly folded it. "I won't be long, Bee, and I'll try not to wake you when I come back."

"Don't worry. I'm sure I'll be out like a light once I've snuggled down."

"Right, well, see you in the morning."

"Yep, goodnight Shell and enjoy the peace and quiet."

As Beatrice snuggled down in her sleeping bag, one hundred and forty miles away, her husband, Brian, entered their marital home in Basingstoke with a pizza box in his hands. Brian had had a wonderful day. He'd caught several good sized fish and had impressed the lads in the pub with the pictures he'd taken as proof.

Once indoors, he locked up and then sat in his favourite armchair to eat his supper. He ate it from the box as he didn't want to dirty a plate and add further to the stack of dirty dishes piling up in the sink. He switched on the television and while he ate watched a news channel because he liked to keep up with current affairs. As he heard about the amber weather warning for heat, he wondered how Beatrice was. Should he give her a ring? He looked at the clock and decided it was too late. He'd ring her in the morning and then afterwards forward her pictures of the fish he'd caught.

Chapter Eight

Down on the beach, Shelley ambled along the water's edge for as far as she could go and then turned around, walked back and sat down on one of the benches. The tide was out and the ambience she considered romantic as the tumbling waves sparkled like jewels in the light of the silvery moon. She leaned back. All was quiet with just the periodical hum of a car travelling through the village and the occasional voice drift from open windows along the sea front.

The sound of the rippling waves was very relaxing and soon Shelley felt her eyelids flickering. Instinctively she removed her cardigan and placed it on the bench for use as a pillow and then wrapped herself in the blanket. Telling herself that she would doze for just a few minutes and then return to the tent, she closed her eyes and listened to the soothing rhythm of waves. But her few minutes' doze was not to be. The three double gin and tonics she had drunk sent her into a deep sleep.

It was just after six when Shelley awoke, dawn had broken and the early morning sun was shining across the calm waters of the high tide. Shocked that she had spent the night sleeping on the beach, she quickly put on her cardigan, folded the blanket and tucked it beneath her arm. As she neared the exit to the main street, she glanced up towards the back of several houses where to her dismay she saw someone watching from the garden of Sea View Cottage. Hoping whoever it was had not recognised her and feeling like a wayward teenager, she dashed along the road towards the Crown and Anchor, fingers crossed that no-one else had seen her.

All was quiet as Shelley ran across the pub field but as she neared the tent she heard voices inside the wigwam. Realising the girls would be getting ready for their early morning warm-up, she quickly unzipped the tent and slipped inside. Beatrice was still asleep. Without undressing, Shelley climbed into her sleeping bag. As she lay awake, she heard the girls leave their wigwam all shushing each other and saying 'be quiet'. They exercised for twenty minutes and then all went silent. Shelley peeped from the tent doorway. The girls had gone. Knowing it was unlikely that she would be able to get back to sleep, she gathered her things together and went for a shower. On leaving the toilet block she filled the kettle from the outside tap and then on her return to the tent, tossed her towel and bag of toiletries inside. She then lit the gas stove ready to make tea. As the water came to the boil, she slipped back inside the tent and picked up their mugs. A quick glance at Beatrice told Shelley that her cousin was still asleep but knowing that she liked to be up by seven she decided to wake her.

"Beatie, time to wake up," Intending to shake her gently, Shelley reached down and touched her cousin's shoulder. It felt cold. She touched her face. It too was cold. Stone cold. Shelley leapt back in horror, reached for her phone and punched in 999.

When the girls returned from their run they were surprised to see an ambulance and a police car on the pub field near to their wigwam. Shelley was sitting in the back of the car talking with a police officer, her eyes red and puffy. To give the police and the emergency services some privacy, James and Ella had invited campers, already up, into the pub where they were given tea and coffee. The four girls, shocked on hearing the news from a police officer, did as suggested and joined the other campers in the bar.

After the ambulance and police left, and the campers returned to the field, Ella guided Shelley inside the pub, poured her a brandy and took her to their private sitting room on the upper floor overlooking the sea. She then sat with her and let her talk about her cousin and how they were the same age and had been friends for as long as she could remember. They had always been close and although they had seen less of each since Beatrice and her husband had moved to Basingstoke, they had kept in touch by social media and frequent phone calls.

"Poor Brian," whispered Shelley.

"Brian?"

"Beat's husband. He'll soon be receiving a visit from the police to tell him about Beatrice. Goodness knows how he'll cope without her," Shelley gave a little laugh. "He likes to pretend he's independent but I don't think he realises just how much Beatrice does around the house. Or should I say, did."

As the clock approached eleven, Shelley stood up. "I'm alright now, Ella. Thank you for your kindness and listening to me but you have a business to run and I refuse to hinder your day's routine."

"Oh, but the business…"

"No, buts, I insist. You've been very good to me and I really appreciate it. But I think the best thing I can do now is go for a short walk to clear my head."

Ella stood. "Are you sure? You're very pale."

"Absolutely sure."

Ella squeezed Shelley's hand. "Well you know where we are if you need someone to talk to."

"Yes, thank you. I appreciate that."

"And don't go too far. It's very hot out there."

"Yes, thank you. I'll probably walk down the nearby lane because it's shady in parts. Beat and I walked down there the other day when we were exploring and followed a bridleway across a field towards the sea."

"Short Lane," said Ella, "an excellent choice. Lots of sprawling sycamore trees and as you say, shade."

The subject of Beatrice's death was the main topic of conversation around the campsite and everyone offered their condolences and told Shelley they would help her in any way they could. The four girls having made plans the previous evening to visit Pentrillick House after lunch asked Shelley if she'd like to join them to take her mind off things. Shelley, touched by their concern, thanked them but said she wanted to be alone and was going for a leisurely walk down Short Lane.

The girls left the village after lunch. They briefly considered walking to Pentrillick House but decided as much as they'd appreciate the exercise it was far too hot and would take too long and so they went in Gretel's car. After walking around the grounds and buying ice creams from a café down by the lake, they booked themselves in for a tour of the house. As they joined the group waiting for the tour to begin, Diane spotted Emma crossing the foyer.

"I recognise you. You were in the pub the other night. The Crown and Anchor."

Emma smiled brightly. "That's right, it's my local."

"Do you work here?" Hannah saw Emma was wearing a name badge indicating that she was the events manager.

"Yes, I do and for that I believe I'm very lucky."

"I'll say. The gardens and grounds are stunning."

"The house is too as you'll see shortly."

"How long does the tour take?" Diane asked.

"Not really sure but about an hour I'd guess."

"Good because we're not in a hurry to get back. Not after what happened to poor Mrs Cookson."

"Mrs Cookson?" Emma was puzzled.

"Yes, she's camping with the author lady on the pub field. At least she was. The poor woman's dead now." Diane's voice shook with emotion.

"Shelley Sinclair," said Gretel. "That's the name of the author, Di."

"Yes, of course. Not that I'd even heard of her before we got here."

"But what happened to her?" Emma asked.

Hannah shrugged her shoulders. "We don't really know much other than the fact Shelley found her dead in the tent this morning. We were out for a run before it got too hot and when we got back there was an ambulance and a police car on the field."

"Oh dear," said Emma, "Perhaps she had health issues and they were made worse by the heat. We've had several people fainting this week."

"Hmm, maybe," said Diane, "but she looked healthy enough and she always has salad with her dinner."

Gretel laughed. "How do you know that, Di?"

"Because I'm nosy, I suppose. No, that's not true. I'm interested in food, diets and what have you and for that reason I notice what people eat and the two ladies in question always ate in the pub's bar rather than the dining room and Mrs Cookson always had salad with whatever and never chips and neither of them ever had a pudding. Unlike the cartoonist chap who always has a pudding and I suspect by her scowls, that his wife very much disapproves."

After their visit to Pentrillick House, the four girls drove over to St. Ives for a look around. While there, they had something to eat and returned to Pentrillick just before nine. Having decided to have a quick drink before they turned in for the night, they went into the pub and the first person they saw was Emma. When they waved to her, Emma walked over to greet them. "So what did you think of Pentrillick House?"

"Wonderful," gushed Hannah, as Diane went to get their drinks.

"Especially the ballroom," said Gretel, "So gracious. I loved it."

"Pleased to hear it. Especially the bit about the ballroom," Emma smiled broadly, "we're having our wedding reception in there next month, you see. The grounds down by the lake are available to hire for weddings and what have you along with a huge marquee but because I work there my bosses are letting us use the ballroom as a wedding present."

"Lucky you," said Gretel."

"Yes, so who are you marrying?" said Hannah as Diane arrived with their drinks.

Emma beckoned Zac, standing with his parents, Aunt Barbara and her husband Jed, over to join them, "Girls, this is my intended, Zac Burton."

"Hi, are you the wigwam girls camping in the field?"

"Wigwam girls, I like that," said Diane, "and yes we are."

"How do you know about us and the wigwam?" Gretel asked.

"My sisters, Kate and Vikki are waitresses here during their holidays and they mentioned the other day that you go out for a run every morning."

"Oh, I know who you mean," said Suzy, "the twins who look very much alike. We must get to know them."

At his home in Basingstoke, Brian Cookson looked around the kitchen after the police left. Empty pizza boxes cluttered the corner work surfaces and the sink was full of dirty dishes. In the washing machine, clothes he'd muddied while out fishing, remained unwashed because he had no idea what the settings and dials on the machine meant. The once spotless white cloth on the kitchen table was stained with coffee rings, tomato ketchup and splashes of beer and an ashtray, brim-full of cigarette butts, stank and needed emptying. The place was a mess and Beatrice had been away for less than a week. He sat down heavily in a chair by the window and looked out onto the gardens his wife had lovingly created. Tears trickled down his cheeks and for the first time in his twenty-one years of marriage he realised what a thoughtless husband he had been. Yet, she had seemed happy enough and never complained. Riddled with guilt for never having taken her on holiday even though she suggested a change of scenery would be nice every year, he vowed to change. Not that change would benefit Beatrice. It was too late for that. Meanwhile, he was faced with the unpleasant task of telling his son and other family members about his and their loss.

Chapter Nine

Because there appeared to be no suspicious circumstances and it was rumoured that Beatrice had complained of too much sun and indigestion, village experts speedily analysed the evidence and concluded that she had died following a heart attack. Therefore everyone was surprised when on Friday afternoon, several police officers arrived at the Crown and Anchor along with scenes of crimes officers.

Ella was out having gone to cash n' carry at the end of lunchtime trade and James was chatting over the bar to Bernie the boatman when the police officers entered the building. Detective Inspector David Bray, the officer in charge, took James to one side and informed him that they needed to interview all members of staff who had worked on Wednesday evening as well as the deceased's cousin, Shelley Sinclair. James readily agreed to help and gave the police the use of his office while he contacted staff who had worked that night and asked them to call in.

Shelley, who was taking a shower when they arrived, was surprised when she stepped out of the shower block to see a police cordon stretched across the entrance to the field. Before she had a chance to query the reason, a police sergeant asked her name and then said they wished to interview her. Although puzzled as she was escorted into the pub, she asked no questions until she was sitting face to face with DI David Bray. When she was told the post mortem revealed that Beatrice's death was not from natural causes, the colour drained from her face. Beatrice it seemed had been poisoned by hemlock.

"What! But how? I mean, how on earth could she have eaten hemlock? It doesn't make sense. I mean, where would she have got it from?"

"That's what we need to find out."

"Well, I'll do what I can to help but if I'm honest I don't know anything about hemlock and I've no idea even what it looks like."

The detective took a sheet of paper from a file and showed Shelley a picture. "This is hemlock. Every bit of the plant is poisonous. One leaf is enough to kill an adult and root tuber would kill a cow. It grows in damp places."

"How can something so pretty be so pernicious?"

The detective nodded and tucked the sheet of paper Shelley had returned to him back in the file. "We've spoken to Mr Dale, the landlord, and he tells us that you and Mrs Cookson both ate here on Wednesday evening. Is that correct?"

"Yes, yes, we did. We've eaten here every night since we arrived on Saturday."

"I see, and may I ask what you ate on Wednesday evening?"

"Of course. We both had the same. A chicken portion with a jacket potato and salad."

"Did Mrs Cookson eat all of her salad?"

"Yes, we both did."

"And she didn't complain about feeling ill?"

"Not ill, no, but she did mention having a touch of indigestion before she went to bed. She felt a bit under the weather too but we put that down to the heat and the fact she'd done quite a bit of walking that day."

"Yes, it has been hot of late, in fact still is. How about you though. Have you felt ill at all?"

"No, no I'm fine."

"Tell me about the meal."

"What do you mean?"

"Where did you sit? Did anyone speak to you as you ate? Did you leave your plates unattended at all?"

"I see. Well, we sat at a table by the piano. The bar was crowded when we arrived but soon after a couple left and so we grabbed their table. A local band was playing, you see, so it was busy and quite noisy even though when we got here the band was taking a break. I don't think we left our meals unattended. No, actually, Beat did. She went to the bar to get more drinks and tell the waitress where we were sitting. You see, when we ordered the food, Tess wrote on the order 'Shell & Beat' because we didn't have a table at the time and planned if we were unable to get one before the food was ready to eat outside. Beatrice could see the waitress had our meals and was obviously looking for us, which as I said is why she approached her. I remained seated while Beat was at the bar and the meals were placed on our table. By then the band was playing again and it was rather noisy."

"And you don't recall anyone passing, or near to your table?"

"No, but…"

"You're frowning, Ms Sinclair. Are you trying to recall something?"

"Yes, I'm just wondering if this might be relevant. You see, with the salad we each had a little dish of dressing. I tipped my dressing on the salad and then scraped out the dish with my finger. When I tasted it I realised I didn't like it because it was very spicy, hot and garlicy. Anyway, Beat thought it was gorgeous and so I shovelled all the salad from my plate that had the dressing on it onto Beat's plate. That just left me with a bit of lettuce, a slice of cucumber and some rocket but I didn't mind and doused it with salad cream."

"And did Mrs Cookson comment on the taste of her salad?"

"Only to say it was gorgeous. She likes spicy stuff, you see. So had there been any hogweed on it I suppose the dressing would have masked it."

The inspector smothered a smile. "Hemlock, Ms Sinclair. Not hogweed. Although hogweed itself is very pernicious and causes nasty burns and blisters if touched."

"Hmm, as you can see, horticulture and stuff like that's not really my thing."

After Shelley, the inspector interviewed bar and kitchen staff who had worked on Wednesday evening. The bar staff were asked if they recalled who sat on the tables in close proximity to Shelley and Beatrice and the kitchen staff were asked if there were any times when the food for the ladies could have been tampered with. Sadly because the bar was busy, people were moving around all the time so the bar staff had no recollection of who sat where. Likewise, the kitchen staff were very busy but were able to confirm that once food was ready to leave the kitchen it always went straight to whoever had ordered it.

Licensees, James and Ella, while eager to help police with their enquiries, were worried the officers might close the pub if they believed it to be a crime scene. They were pleased therefore when they were told to carry on as usual but to be vigilant. For although it was possible Beatrice's food may have been tampered with on the premises, there was nothing to back this up. The kitchen and public bar had been cleaned several times since the death occurred and therefore there was nothing for forensics to scrutinise.

"Rum do about that poor woman," said Layton, in for a drink at the Crown and Anchor with retired DI Paul Fox later that evening. "Needless to say I'm pretty hot on the subject of horticulture but I've never known anyone to be poisoned by hemlock. Dreadful stuff though. It ought to be destroyed."

"Yes, it's not something I've come across in my career, I must admit. Be it accidental or deliberate."

"You think it might have been deliberate then?"

"It's possible but I should imagine unless anyone witnessed anything untoward it'd be impossible to say one way or another."

"Well, let's hope it was accidental. I don't like the thought of a murderer in our midst."

"Me neither." Paul glanced around the bar, "I'm surprised our four ladies aren't here tonight. I'd have thought the news of Mrs Cookson's death being suspicious would have got them here sniffing around eager to know the latest."

"Perhaps they've not heard yet or they prefer the comfort of their own home on these warm summer nights."

"Would have to be the former because they'd happily forgo the comfort of their homes if they knew there was a mystery to fathom out."

Layton raised his hand. "Talking of homes, I'm thinking of having my sitting room decorated and wonder if you know of any local tradesmen who might be up for the job."

"Without hesitation I'd say Norman Williams. He decorated my flat and I was very pleased with his work. Drink up and I'll ask Jackie since she's working on the bar tonight. Jackie shares a home with him, you see, and because Norman's coming up for retirement age there's a chance he might not be taking on any more jobs."

Jackie Paige was Norman's twenty-four year old lodger. Previously they had been next-door neighbours in Dawlish where Jackie lived with her parents and Norman lived with his elderly widowed mother. They became good friends when Jackie and her mother helped Norman to look after his mother in the last months of her life. It was after his mother's death that Norman looked into his past and Jackie who had an interest in ancestry had helped him. This led them to Cornwall where Norman discovered his roots and eventually decided to retire to Pentrillick, the village of his birth. Because Jackie had made friends in the village during their visit she asked if she might go with him as a paying lodger and Norman readily agreed.

They moved into one of the new houses at Cobblestone Close in 2019 just before Christmas and straight away Jackie secured a job at the Crown and Anchor where she assisted the chef or worked on the bar. Norman meanwhile, who then had a few years to go before he qualified for his state pension, decided to do a bit of painting and decorating. It was something he enjoyed and was good at.

When asked, Jackie confirmed that Norman was still taking on work and said to give him a ring. He was home at present watching a film on the television.

At Primrose Cottage, unaware of the latest developments, feeling tired after a day in the charity shop and from spending half an hour watering the garden after dinner, Hetty and Lottie decided to stay at home and watch Gardeners' World rather than go to the pub. Having learned from a customer while in the shop that eight out of fourteen regions in England were in drought status and that Devon and Cornwall was one of the eight, the sisters were feeling rather dejected.

Hetty glanced from the window at the dying blue flowers on a wilting hydrangea in the front garden. "Hosepipe bans before long, I suppose."

"Oh don't," muttered Lottie, as she turned on the television, "Takes me right back to 1976."

Hetty sat down. "Horrible, wasn't it? Remember how we were on the verge of having standpipes back in Northants and other places too of course. What a nightmare."

"It was but I don't think it'll be as bad as that. At least I hope not."

Chapter Ten

"Have you heard the latest?" Kitty gushed, red in the face and pausing to regain her breath after speed-walking up the hill from the village.

It was Saturday morning and Hetty and Lottie were in their front garden, weeding, hoeing and deadheading.

"No, well, nothing that would account for the look on your face, that is." Hetty knew from experience that Kitty, placid by nature, only showed signs of excitement when something extraordinary had happened.

"Unless it's we're getting standpipes." Lottie dropped the empty washing up bowl on the path having tipped its contents around the base of the wilting hydrangea.

"Standpipes! Good heavens, no. Nothing like that, thank goodness."

Hetty removed her gardening gloves and dropped them in a bucket of weeds. "Come in then and tell us what the latest is. You look like you need to sit down."

"Thank you, I'm sweating buckets." Kitty entered the garden, removed her sunhat and used it to fan her face. "The news is about that Beatrice lady. You know, the one who was on holiday with that Shelley person and died." The sisters nodded. "Well, according to the village jungle drums, she didn't die from natural causes, she was poisoned and by hemlock, would you believe? What's more, the police don't think she ate it accidently, which means they must think she was murdered."

"What! But why and by whom? As far as we know she hardly knew anyone here." Hetty was verging on speechless.

67

"Come on. Let's get the kettle on and you can tell us all you know, Kitty. It'll be nice to get out of the sun anyway." Lottie picked up the empty washing up bowl and led the way into the house.

When all had coffee and were seated in the sitting room, Kitty began to explain.

"I heard about it in the post office. Several people were in there and it's all anyone was talking about. Apparently, the police were at the pub yesterday afternoon questioning everyone and Shelley in particular. Rumour has it that the poison may have been added to the salad Beatrice ate in the pub and I know the pub staff have all been questioned because Tess was there working on the bar last night and she told Marlene when she saw her out jogging this morning and Marlene was the one who kicked the gossip into action when she went to the post office for whatever reason." Kitty stopped talking to catch her breath, "Silly woman. Marlene, that is. She reckons the person who killed Beatrice has a grudge against dinner ladies and feels she might be the next victim. Such a drama queen."

Hetty tutted. "Isn't she just? Still, that's why she always takes the lead in the drama group's productions."

Lottie suddenly threw up her hands. "If the police questioned everyone who was working in the pub that night, were Kate and Vicki amongst them?"

"Yes, but so were Jade and Juliet who Tess said are really upset. Apparently it was Jade who took out the meals to Beatrice and Shelley but it was Juliet who arranged the salad on their plates."

"Oh no. Poor girls."

"So it's reckoned the poison used was hemlock," mused Hetty. "I'm not even sure I know what that looks like or where it grows."

"You would if you saw it, Het," Lottie assured her. "It's a bit like cow parsley and grows in damp shady places but can be found in wasteland and in ditches too."

"Very much so," Kitty agreed, "but if you look closely you can tell them apart. Hemlock's leaves are darker than cow parsley's and it has purple blotches on its stems. I know the difference because it's something my dad drummed into me many years ago."

"But surely you'd have to eat an awful lot of it to kill you," said Hetty.

Kitty shook her head. "No, not at all. Every part of the plant is poisonous and just one leaf is enough to kill a person. Especially someone petite like poor Beatrice was."

"Meanwhile, Shelley is still here," said Lottie. "I'm surprised. I think if I were in her shoes I'd want to get as far away as possible."

"She is, and as I said the police questioned her yesterday. What's more I should imagine they have asked her to stay. Insisted even. After all, she's the last person to see Beatrice alive and the only one in Pentrillick who really knew her."

Lottie gasped. "But surely she's not a suspect?"

Kitty shrugged her shoulders. "Who knows? I mean, she might have done it to see the effects so that she can use it in her next book, although that would be a bit extreme."

"So it would," agreed Hetty. "She'd have to be very silly to think she'd get away with it."

"We need to speak with her," said Lottie, "and as soon as possible."

Hetty placed her empty coffee mug on the floor. "Good idea. We'll go to the pub tonight and if she's not in we'll pop along to her tent and see her there."

"She's not in her tent," said Kitty. "It's a crime scene now and so surrounded by police tape. In fact all the campers have been told to move their tents, caravans and so forth further down the field. Even Harry and his mates have had to move out of the static caravan and they're sleeping on the floor in Ella and James' sitting room."

"So where is Shelley then?" Lottie asked.

"In the pub. Fortunately someone left yesterday and so they've a room free until Monday. It's reckoned by then the forensic lot will have finished their work and everyone will be allowed to spread out again."

"We can't go to the pub tonight, Het. Remember, Barbara and Jed are taking us all out for a meal to celebrate their marriage."

"Damn! I'd forgotten that. It'll have to be tomorrow then. Will you join us, Kitty?"

"Definitely, but it won't be 'til after Evensong. It's not my turn to play the organ but I'm down to read a lesson."

"Ideal: we'll plan to be there around half seven then. Meanwhile, I'll ring Debbie, put her in the picture and get her to be there too."

On Saturday afternoon, as arranged over the phone, Norman Williams called at Saltwater House to price up the decorating job in Layton's sitting room. On arrival, Norman knocked on the front door of the house and Layton promptly answered.

"Ah, I know who you are now. I've seen you in the pub on several occasions." Layton warmly shook Norman's hand.

"Likewise, I've seen you too but have never had reason to introduce myself." Norman stepped over the threshold and closed the door behind him.

"I'll show you the room I want done and if it's agreeable we'll pop in the kitchen afterwards and have a coffee and a chat as long as you're not in a hurry to get away, that is."

"Sounds good and no, I don't have to dash away for anything." Norman followed Layton down a long hallway and into a brightly lit room with sea views. After discussing what needed doing, a price was agreed and Norman said he'd start the job on Monday after he'd been to the builders for supplies. The two men then went back along the hallway and into a large kitchen. Standing on top of a fridge looking out of the window, was the African grey parrot.

"Clarence, meet Norman," said Layton.

Clarence turned his head. "Where's Lottie?"

"Lottie's not coming to see us today. Say hello to Norman."

"Norman," said Clarence and resumed his observation from the window.

"I take it he likes Lottie," Norman sat down at the table after Layton pulled out a chair for him.

"Like! He's besotted with her but he's not so keen on Hetty or their friends Debbie and Kitty."

"He's a bit choosy then."

"I'll say he is. Over the years I've had lots of lady friends and he's disliked them all. That's one of the reasons I never married. Well, that and the fact I've never felt like taking the plunge. How about you, Norman. Are you married?"

"No, and like you I never have been."

"Where's Lottie?"

"Shush, Clarence. She's not coming round today." Layton turned to Norman: "Lottie's teaching me to knit so pops in several times a week."

"Knit! What as in with needles and wool?"

"The only type I know of and your reaction's much like mine. It all started, you see, when I heard that the chap camping on the pub field in a camper van, taught knitting. I mentioned it to the ladies in the pub one night and foolishly referred to him as a pansy. Lottie took me to task and said I ought to try it as it's very therapeutic. I said I wouldn't know where to start and she offered to teach me. And the rest as they say, is history."

"And do you like it?"

"Love it. I've started off with a simple scarf and if it meets with approval I'll be working on a pullover next. I've been pretty active all my life and it's rewarding to do something productive while sitting down taking my ease."

"Hmm, not my thing but I can see your point and it's good to have a hobby, which makes me ask, is that painting one of the ex-detective inspector's? It's just the signature looks familiar."

"Yes, it is. When I heard Paul was into painting, I asked him if he'd do one of my house. He said yes, and as you can see it's pretty impressive. He usually does boats but welcomed a change and is going to concentrate more on buildings from now on."

"Very nice too. He's a talented chap."

Layton made the coffee, placed a bowl of sugar on the table and then sat down opposite Norman. Simultaneously, a smooth-haired Dachshund waddled into the room and sat down by Layton's chair.

"A sausage dog," chuckled Norman. "What's his name?"

Layton reached down and stroked the dog's soft fur. "George. He's getting old now so doesn't have the energy he did when he was a pup. Which is probably just as well because neither do I."

"Snap."

"Where's Lottie?" asked Clarence.

"Probably home with Hetty," said Norman, seeing that Layton wasn't going to answer.

"Hetty," Clarence banged his beak against the window. "Where's Lottie?"

"Do these two get on?" Norman asked.

"Oh, yes, although Clarence is inclined to tease George. His favourite spot is up there on top of the fridge so he can see out of the window. He's a wonderful mimic and when he sees George outside he imitates my whistle to a T. George then comes running in expecting to be fed and Clarence laughs. Cheeky so and so."

In the afternoon as the church clock struck four, a Ford Mustang pulled up in the parking area alongside Sea View Cottage. From the driver's seat stepped a man in his late sixties and from the passenger seat his wife of a similar age. From the back they removed two suitcases and entered the cottage by the conservatory door where the key was hidden beneath a terracotta pot of petunias.

Betsy Triggs who was unpegging her washing from the line in the back garden of the house next door when they arrived, greeted them over the garden fence and wished them a pleasant holiday. Betsy, an elderly widow who lived alone, then returned indoors with her washing basket relieved that the latest visitors were just two in number and unlikely to be rowdy. Not that many of Sea View's visitors were rowdy. Most were very friendly and no trouble at all. In fact Betsy liked living next door to a holiday cottage because her neighbours changed frequently.

Chapter Eleven

Although distraught by the death of her cousin, Shelley had no desire to return home to Canterbury; furthermore, she had been instructed by the police, as Kitty suggested, to remain in the area should they wish to question her further. She was, however, a little nervous for at the back of her mind a nagging voice kept telling her that the police saw her as a potential suspect and the notion terrified her.

Inside her temporary room at the Crown and Anchor, looking for her hairbrush, she shuffled through a few of her belongings which the police had allowed her to remove from the tent. As she slowly brushed her hair she pondered over the last evening she and Beatrice had spent together. If the salad had been tampered with, as was suspected, then could she have been the intended victim? After all the hemlock leaves were most likely on her plate and amongst the salad the bulk of which she had passed over to Beatrice. It was an alarming thought but more than feasible. Shelley sat down on the bed and attempted to recall who if anyone had passed by their table but the memory was a blur. The corner where they had sat was dimly lit and because of the band playing there were people all around. Then of course it was possible that the food was tampered with before it reached their table. She knew the kitchen staff had been questioned but could see no reason why anyone in there would have wanted to poison either herself or Beatrice as neither of them knew the kitchen staff. If fact neither of them really knew anyone in Cornwall at all, so who on earth could have wanted either of them dead? Perhaps then it had been an accident and Beatrice had picked it up somewhere unknowingly. The police obviously saw that as a possibility otherwise why would they be going through the tent with a fine toothcomb? Then there was the fact Beatrice had spent several hours in Penzance. Had she eaten something dodgy there? After all she said she would have lunch in town. She decided to mention it to the police even though she had no idea what Beatrice might have eaten or where.

On Sunday evening, feeling peckish, Shelley went downstairs for something to eat and ate in the dining room where there were fewer people. Since it had become known that Beatrice's death was no longer from natural causes, she felt sure that fingers would be pointing in her direction from both locals and holidaymakers. For that reason she had stayed in her room the previous evening watching television and saw no-one except Ella, who after insisting she ate something, called in with a plate of vegetable chilli and rice.

After her meal, she left the dining room and peeped into the bar. Should she risk going in for a drink or should she return to her room? She looked at her watch; it was a quarter to nine. Too early to turn in for the night; there was nothing she wanted to watch on the television and she was certainly not in the mood for writing. With a sudden boost of confidence she walked into the bar, head held high. She was after all innocent of any wrong doing and should she be accused thus she would stand her ground.

After buying a drink, she looked around the bar for somewhere to sit. To her delight, four ladies sat around a table and beckoned her to join them.

"You look a bit lost without your cousin," said a kindly voice. "We'd be delighted to have your company." Lottie pulled out a chair for the author.

Shelley sat down gratefully. "Thank you. We've met before, haven't we?" She looked at Lottie: "Your daughter is married to that dashingly handsome American police officer."

"That's right, she is. I'm Lottie, by the way. We didn't introduce ourselves the other evening, did we?"

"No you didn't but I know Hetty's name because we're now friends on Facebook."

"That's right and I'm Lottie's twin sister. These other two ladies are our good friends, Debbie and Kitty." Hetty waved her hand to the ladies in turn.

"Delighted to meet you all and you know who I am from the other night."

"Yes," said Debbie, "and we're so sorry about the death of your cousin. She seemed a lovely lady."

"Yes, she was."

Kitty, noting tears welling in Shelley's eyes attempted to change the subject. "It's really nice to meet you again although we have to confess that until we met you the other night we'd never heard of you."

Shelley laughed. "You're not alone there. I have a modest following for which I'm very grateful and my work brings me in an adequate income but I'll never be a best seller."

"You might be one day. None of us knows what lays round the corner," said Hetty.

"True. Poor old Beat certainly didn't."

"Was your cousin married?" Debbie asked.

"Yes, she was married to Brian. He's a nice enough chap but perhaps a bit lazy. Beat did everything for him but then I think that's the way she liked it. You know, she liked to mother him. It made her feel needed."

"Any children?" Hetty was curious.

"Just the one, a son, Marc. He doesn't live at home, he shares a small place with his girlfriend in Faversham so he's only a few miles from me. He's a lovely lad and he'll be devastated to have lost his mum because him being an only child they were very close."

"So do your family come from Kent?" Debbie asked.

"Yes, Beat's mum and my mum were sisters and they grew up in Canterbury. After they married, Beat's parents moved to Faversham and they're still there. My parents stayed in Canterbury and died a few years back. I'm still living in the house I grew up in having bought my brother out when we inherited the place."

"So you have a brother," calculated Debbie.

"Yes, Steve. He's a couple of years younger than me and has a good job with the council. He and his wife have a grown up son who having just finished university, still lives with them."

"And where did Beatrice live?" Hetty asked.

"Beat moved to Basingstoke soon after she married Brian. Marc grew up there of course but moved up to Faversham a year or so ago. He and his girlfriend currently live in a granny annexe at the home of his grandparents; they being Beat's mum and dad."

"Sounds complicated," said Debbie.

"It's not really and I suppose it doesn't matter anyway."

"I hope you don't think us insensitive," said Hetty, "but the four of us like solving mysteries especially if it involves a murder. So needless to say, we're keen to find out just what happened to your cousin."

Shelley half smiled. "Are you any good?"

"Well, umm…I'm not quite sure how to answer that."

Shelley was clearly interested. "Why don't we meet up for a chat during the daytime? I'd love to hear more but it's a bit noisy in here and I'm starting to feel rather weary. I've not been sleeping too well, you see."

"That's understandable," sympathised Kitty.

"Why don't you come up to our place," said Lottie. "It's not far from here and we can all meet for a chat over coffee."

"Sounds wonderful and with Beat gone I'm free every day."

"Let's make it Tuesday then," said Hetty, eagerly, "I'd say tomorrow but Lottie and I work in the charity shop on Mondays, Wednesdays and Fridays."

"Yes, that sounds fine to me. I have to move out of my room here and back into my tent in the morning and then I need to go shopping so Tuesday would suit me fine."

"Perfect," said Lottie, "Let's aim for eleven o'clock shall we?"

Everyone agreed and Shelley was given directions to Primrose Cottage.

"And since you showed interest in it the other day, we'll take the crystal ball home with us after work tomorrow as well," said Hetty.

"The one you saw my name in. Yes, I'd very much like to see that." Shelley finished her drink and then stood up. "I'm sure you ladies won't mind if I make my exit now but I'd like to get to bed and try to get a decent night's sleep before returning to my old camp bed."

"Of course we don't mind," said Lottie, "and we'll see you on Tuesday."

As Shelley left for the guest rooms upstairs, Layton arrived with glass in hand. "Ah, my favourite ladies. May I join you?"

"Of course," they replied in unison.

Layton happily sat in the chair vacated by Shelley and moved it closer to Lottie. "Was that lady you were talking to the one whose cousin has died?" he asked.

"Yes," said Hetty with enthusiasm, "and we're meeting up with her on Tuesday when we hope to learn more of their circumstances."

"Meeting up with who?" Retired DI Paul Fox grabbed a vacant chair from the next table and placed it between Hetty and Debbie.

"The lady whose cousin was murdered," said Layton seeing none of the four ladies seemed willing to enlighten him.

Paul tutted. "I hope you're not intending to poke your noses in where they're not wanted." He took a sip of his beer and glanced at the four ladies in turn.

"As if..." Hetty was unable to finish the sentence knowing that was precisely what they intended to do.

"These ladies can be troublesome," he said to Layton, "so best keep an eye on them otherwise they might get up to mischief."

Chapter Twelve

When Shelley woke inside her room at the Crown and Anchor on Monday morning she was relieved to see the day was dull and a few spots of rain were visible on the pavement below her window. And although the rain came to nothing she knew at least that the drop in temperature would mean sleeping in the tent would be less uncomfortable than the nights prior to her cousin's death.

Feeling better following her chat with the ladies the previous evening she went down to breakfast with a spring in her step; after which, she moved out of her room so that it could be cleaned and prepared for people arriving later in the day.

Out in the field, she was pleased to see the girls' wigwam back beside her own tent and because some of the windows in the static caravan were part-open she assumed that it was occupied once again by Harry and his two friends. After settling down she wandered through the village to the beach where on impulse she paddled in the sea. As she sat on a bench waving her feet to dry them, Claude Dexter, the MP's husband, stepped onto the beach from the cliff path that led to and passed by The Old Lifeboat House.

"Mind if I join you? I'm on my way to the shop for milk but it's a fair old trek from where we're staying in the Old Lifeboat House and I could do with resting my legs for five minutes."

Shelley ceased waving her feet and tucked them neatly beneath the bench. "Be my guest. A bit of company is always appreciated and you have a friendly face."

"Thank you. I don't think anyone's ever said that to me before."

Their brief conversation was mainly about Shelley, her work, with which, to her surprise, he was familiar, and the tragic death of Beatrice. Claude, with a good bedside manner, was sympathetic and understanding. His words, Shelley found were a great comfort and they parted vowing to speak again before their holidays ended. On the way back to the campsite Shelley called in at the pasty shop for some lunch and to her delight, Eve, Dolly and young Dee were equally sympathetic.

In the afternoon, as planned, she drove to Penzance for a few groceries; as she passed a display of chilli sausages in the supermarket, she remembered the disposable barbecue she had purchased from the beach shop and so bought sausages, a crusty roll and a small tub of coleslaw. She also bought a bottle of chardonnay to cheer herself up, making sure the one she chose had a screw top.

On arriving back at the campsite, she was amused to see the wigwam girls kicking around a football at the far end of the field. When they had finished and wandered back to their temporary home, Shelley was carefully placing stones outside her tent and attempting to make their top level. On hearing their voices she looked up. "I'm very impressed with you girls because I've never known young ladies as keen on sport and exercise as you four are."

"Got to keep Hannah in practice," said Gretel, who Shelley knew to be a fitness instructor.

"Really, and why's that?"

Hannah giggled. "Because I'm not only a trainee PE teacher but also an aspiring semi-professional footballer and I'm determined to get to the top and play for England one day. Mind you, I need to improve a lot first."

Shelley smiled. "Motivated no doubt by the ladies' success in the Euro's thing."

"Precisely."

"Well good luck. As they say, practice makes perfect."

"It certainly does. I'm loads better than I was this time last year."

"So if you're a footballer-cum-PE teacher, Hannah, and you Gretel are a fitness instructor, what do you other two do?"

"Nothing quite as awesome I'm, afraid," said Diane, "I'm a beauty consultant and Suzy here is a hair stylist."

"Nothing wrong with those professions, girls. It's nice to be pampered and I'd be lost without my hairdresser."

Hannah tilted her head to one side. "Please don't think I'm being nosy, but what are you trying to do with those stones?"

Shelley chuckled. "I'm attempting to make a flat surface to put my disposable barbecue on but I'm not doing very well because the stones are odd shapes and too small. I must persevere though because I can't have my sausages rolling off onto the grass."

"Why don't you use the bricks?"

Shelley looked up at Hannah. "Bricks? What bricks?"

"The ones at the back of the car park. There's a notice beside them saying they're for use by campers for disposable barbecues. I'll go and get you some." Hannah ran off bouncing the football as she crossed the field. Within minutes she was back with six bricks. "Will this be enough?"

"Yes, that's perfect. Thank you so much. I need to keep my eyes open in future because I hadn't seen them or the notice." Shelley picked up the odd-shaped stones and dropped them back beneath the hedge where she had found them while Hannah neatly arranged the bricks.

In the early evening, Shelley went for a stroll through the village and onto the beach to get some fresh air. For she reasoned the more fresh air she had the better she might sleep. When she returned to the campsite she took out her garden chair from the back of her car, unfolded it and placed it on the grass. She then fetched the disposable barbecue from inside the tent and stood it on the bricks arranged by Hannah so that the barbecue did not scorch the grass, already discoloured through lack of rain. As she opened the bottle of wine, she realised that she didn't have a glass and so went into the pub.

"I know it's a bit cheeky, Ella, but could I borrow a glass. I've bought a bottle of wine you, see, to drink while I barbecue some sausages but I've nothing to drink it in. Well actually that's not quite true, I have a mug but I'm sure it wouldn't taste half as nice in that as it would in a glass."

"Of course, Shelley. We're only too glad to do anything to help," she reached for a glass and passed it across the bar, "and I must say it's nice to see a bit of colour back in your face."

"Thank you. I went to Penzance this afternoon because I needed to get away for a while. I'm sure it helped because I'm feeling a bit better. I've got over the shock and now I'm beginning to grieve. It's very difficult though because I feel so guilty and it's probably not a good idea, but I bought the bottle of wine to drown my sorrows. Of course it would help if I had some inclination as to who was responsible for Beat's death. As it is I can't think of even one suspect," she attempted to laugh, "which is pretty poor going for someone who makes a modest living writing murder mystery books."

"Well, I'm sure the police are doing their best."

"I hope so but I've a sneaky feeling that they like me are baffled as to what might have been the motive. On the other hand, perhaps it was an accident, in which case we'll never know how or why."

Ella watched as Shelley picked up the glass. "I'm sure I don't need to ask you to be careful with the barbecue. You know, the risk of fire and all that."

"Don't worry, I'll be very vigilant and not leave it unattended. My late grandfather, on Mum's side of the family, was a fireman and fire safety was drilled into us from a very early age."

Back on the field, Shelley poured a glass of wine, lit the barbecue, sat down on her garden chair and watched the world go by. There was not a breath of wind and from her place of observation, she was able to see people going in and out of the pub, watch its clientele eating and drinking in the gardens, see children in the play area and other campers sitting outside their temporary homes. As Shelley finished her glass of wine, she tested the barbecue for heat. Happy that it was hot enough she placed the sausages on the grill and poured another drink. Watching a cluster of fluffy pink clouds amongst the grey, she thought of Beatrice and wondered how Brian would cope without his wife. She thought about the plot for her next book; something she had not considered since her cousin's death, and then she thought about the ladies she was to visit the following day. They had been sympathetic over her loss as had everyone, and she looked forward to chatting with them in their home and seeing for herself, the crystal ball.

Harry, Jake and Jack returned to the campsite just after eleven that evening having been out for the day in Newquay, surfing.

"Shall we have a barbecue? Remember we bought two disposables the other day and haven't used one yet. We've still got a few cans of beer as well." The smell of bacon frying inside Happy's camper van made Jake feel hungry.

"But we haven't got anything to barbecue," laughed Jack, as Harry unlocked the caravan door, "although I must admit I am starving."

"Oh, bugger. Didn't think of that."

"No problem. You two go in and get the barbecue and beer; I'll go and scrounge some burgers from the pub." Harry tossed the caravan keys onto the table and dashed off towards the pub's entrance. When he arrived back on the field he found his friends sitting on one of the picnic benches.

"We've come over here so we can put the barbecue on the path. Don't want to scorch you folks' grass even though it already looks dead."

"Good thinking. I forgot to say there are bricks in the car park for barbecues but the path will do just as well," Harry placed a bag containing rolls on the table, and a plate on which lay three half-pound burgers, he then sat down.

"It's a bit eerie being out here this time of night," said Jake, "especially knowing there's a murderer on the loose. I mean he could be watching us and we'd be none the wiser."

"Just as well we're not having any salad then," Harry opened a can of lager and drank half in one go.

"I have to agree about it being eerie though," said Jack, "I mean, I know it's not ever so late but the campsite seems so quiet. Apart from Happy frying his bacon I reckon everyone else has turned in for the night."

"I bet the girls haven't," Jake finished his can of beer and opened another.

Jack shook his head. "No, I reckon they will have. Remember they get up at silly o'clock every morning for a warm-up and then they go for a run."

"They can't be in the pub anyway," said Harry, "because it's closed now and my folks and Tess are in there clearing up."

Jake frowned. "I thought the girls were supposed to be on holiday."

"It's a fitness holiday apparently," laughed Jack, "Whatever that means. I was chatting to one of them the other day. Suzy I think she said her name was and she's a hairdresser. Anyway, she said they have to be in bed by ten and up by half past five."

Harry waved his hand over the barbecue to test it for heat. "In that case I'd better put these burgers on or we'll still be sitting here when they get up."

Chapter Thirteen

During the night, two bursts of heavy rain fell over Pentrillick and inhabitants woke the following morning to find the roads glistening and water dripping from shrivelled leaves.

Hetty, first up in Primrose Cottage, stepped outside to relish the welcome dampness and take in a breath of the fresh clean air.

"Shelley couldn't have had a worse night to go back under canvas," she said when Lottie stepped out to join her, "Did you hear the rain in the night? I actually had to get out of bed and close the windows it was so heavy."

As the sisters sat drinking tea, Barbara and Jed joined them in the living room having made themselves mugs of coffee in the kitchen.

"You might need umbrellas today," said Lottie, "although didn't you say you were going shopping?"

Barbara sat down. "Yes, we're going to Truro where I hear they had flash floods yesterday."

"I heard mention of that but we didn't have a drop during the day here, did we, Het?"

"No, more's the shame. Still, hopefully it'll rain all day today and top the reservoirs up, but I doubt it."

At half past ten, after Barbara and Jed had left for Truro, Lottie welcomed Kitty to Primrose Cottage.

"I thought I'd get here early because I didn't want to miss anything if Shelley got here before me," Kitty handed Lottie a cherry cake freshly baked that morning, "I see Debbie's car's not outside so assume she's not here yet."

"Yes, I am," a voice called from the sitting room, "I walked so I could relish the fresh smell after the rain."

Lottie closed the front door as Kitty went into the sitting room and sat down beside Debbie on the sofa.

"Where's Hetty?" Kitty asked when Lottie entered the sitting room.

"In the bathroom cleaning the wash basin. Having the taps glistening is a fetish of hers and she wants to create a good impression." Lottie sat down.

"I wonder how Shelley slept now she's back in the tent," Kitty shuddered, "Rather her than me."

"Not very well I should imagine," said Debbie, "The rain on canvas must be deafening."

"Het and I were saying that this morning and we've decided to tell her that she's welcome to our single room here if she's fed up with sleeping in a tent."

Debbie chuckled. "She'll like that alright with Jed staying here too."

"That's what Het said. Anyway, we'll wait and see."

"Where are Barbara and Jed?"

"They've gone to Truro to get Zac and Emma a wedding present."

"Tommy and I have decided to give them money," said Kitty, "because already having their own place I've no idea what they'll need."

"We're doing the same," said Debbie.

Lottie nodded. "So are we but Barbara wants to get them a coffee making thingy. She hates instant coffee, you see, and says no-one should have to drink it."

"You've a coffee maker haven't you?" Debbie asked.

"Yes, we have. When we first had it we used it all the time but then we got lazy, went back to instant and it ended up in a cupboard. Needless to say it's out again now though because Barbara can't function until she's had several mugs in the morning and Jed's much the same."

By eleven o'clock, Hetty was back with the ladies, the coffee maker was on and they sat patiently awaiting their guest. They chatted as they waited, casually glancing at the clock as the minutes ticked by. At twenty minutes past eleven Hetty stood up and crossed to the window. "Do you think she's got lost?"

"I don't see how," said Debbie, "there's only one lane opposite the pub and it leads here. You'd have to be pretty daft not to be able to find us."

"That's what I was thinking." Hetty sat back down, "and we can't ask the crystal ball because we forgot to bring it home with us after work yesterday."

"Does anyone have her mobile number?" Lottie asked.

Debbie and Kitty shook their heads.

Hetty picked her phone up from the coffee table. "I don't have her number but we are friends on Facebook so I'll send her a message."

With the message sent the ladies patiently waited for a reply but the message remained unread and Shelley was not on-line.

Hetty stood up. "Well, I'm going to have a coffee before it spoils. How about the rest of you?"

All said they'd like coffee too and Debbie went with Hetty to the kitchen to help carry the four mugs.

Ten more minutes passed. The message remained unread and still there was no sign of Shelley.

"Something's not right," Hetty leaned over the arm of her chair and placed her empty mug on the hearth slate.

"Perhaps she can't make it for some reason and she can't phone because her battery's flat. After all she can't charge it in a tent, can she?" Lottie jumped as the clock struck twelve.

"Good point," said Kitty, "Shall we go down to the village to see if we can find her?"

"Yes, I think we ought," Debbie stood up and eased her back.

"I hope she's not been arrested for Beatrice's murder," Lottie's comment came out of the blue.

"No! Surely not," gasped Kitty, "I mean what could be her motive?"

Lottie shrugged her shoulders. "I don't know but it's possible, isn't it? I mean she certainly had the opportunity."

"Well, there's only one way to find out and it's to do as Kitty suggested and try and find her." Hetty removed her slippers and reached for her shoes.

All agreed and so they locked up the house and walked down Long Lane towards the village. To give him a walk, they took Albert with them. As they reached the pub and stepped onto the field they could see Shelley's Morris Traveller beside her tent.

"Well, if she's out she can't have gone far," reasoned Debbie.

When they reached Shelley's tent they saw the zip was fastened. Lottie tapped on the canvas. "Are you in there, Shelley?"

There was no reply.

"Perhaps she's gone for a walk," said Kitty.

"But why when she said she was coming to visit us." Hetty felt quite annoyed.

"I wouldn't be surprised if Lottie's not right and she's been arrested," said Debbie, "I mean, she wouldn't have taken her car if that were the case."

"True, so shall we go in the pub and ask if anyone knows where she is?" Kitty looked around the field, "I mean, none of the other campers are here to ask."

"I'm just going to check she's not in her tent first," Hetty passed Albert's lead to Kitty.

"But why? She didn't answer when I knocked," tutted Lottie.

"Because I have a nasty feeling, that's why." Hetty unzipped the tent, peeped inside and then jumped back in alarm.

90

"What is it, Het?" Lottie noted her sister's face was devoid of colour.

Hetty couldn't speak.

Debbie took hold of the tent flap and looked inside. Shelley lay on her camp bed perfectly still. Fearing the worst, Debbie crept forward and touched Shelley's bright red face. It was stone cold. Realising she was dead, Debbie slowly stepped away. As she moved backwards towards the tent's entrance, she tripped over something on the floor. It was a disposable barbecue.

Chapter Fourteen

Having purchased the wedding gift for Zac and Emma, Barbara and Jed mulled over whether to have lunch in Truro or return to Pentrillick to eat at the Crown and Anchor. Barbara was keen to find somewhere in Truro but knowing that Jed was eager to sample something on the Crown and Anchor's 'specials' board she suggested they return to Pentrillick. As they approached the pub and turned into the car park they were surprised to see several police cars and an ambulance on the field. There was also a police officer at the entrance to the pub field preventing access. They were even more surprised when they saw Lottie, Hetty, Debbie and Kitty being questioned by officers.

"Mum," gasped Barbara, "what's going on? Why is she speaking with the police?"

Nearby, amongst the bystanders watching the activity on the field was Happy Harper who heard Barbara's comment.

"It's the author lady. She's been found dead in her tent."

"What! You mean Shelley Sinclair?"

"Yes."

"But she was supposed to be visiting Mum, Auntie Het and their friends today. They were quite excited about it. Any idea what happened?"

"Not really, but I overheard one of the coppers say something about suicide."

"No, surely not."

Jed placed his arm around his wife's shoulders. "These things happen, Barbara, and the death of her cousin might well have affected her more than anyone realised."

Barbara watched as police erected a white tent at the entrance of a smaller one. "Yes, makes sense, I suppose, but why are Mum, Auntie Het, Debbie and Kitty there?"

"I don't know," Jed turned to Happy, "Do you know why those ladies are being questioned?" He pointed to Barbara's mother, aunt and their friends.

"Because they found her. I was in my van at the time getting ready to go down to the beach. I heard lots of shouting and then when I came out I could see they were upset about something and one of them was on her phone. I asked what was wrong and they told me. The police arrived shortly after and everyone not involved was asked to leave the field."

An hour later, the police told the ladies they could go and Jed and Barbara concerned for their welfare offered to escort them back to Primrose Cottage. However, Lottie assured them they were fine and insisted they carry on doing whatever they planned to do. Admitting they were hungry, Barbara and Jed went into the Crown and Anchor for lunch saying they would catch up with them after. The ladies, wanting time to think, walked back to Primrose Cottage in silence, all deep in thought. When fresh coffee was brewed, rounds of sandwiches made and Kitty's cherry cake sliced, they sat round the dining table to eat and try to make sense of what little they knew.

"Well my opinion, for what it's worth, is there's no way it was suicide," Lottie was adamant, "I mean we only saw her on Sunday night and she seemed quite perky then."

"Yes, but we don't know what happened yesterday," reasoned Debbie, "Going back in the tent might have triggered horrible memories and it got the better of her."

"And if it wasn't suicide, why on earth would she have taken the barbecue inside her tent," said Hetty, "She cooked with it outside so it makes no sense."

"How do you know she cooked outside?" Kitty asked, "I mean, no doubt she did but you never know."

"Because there were six bricks outside her tent which I assume she'd put there to prevent the grass from looking worse than it already does. Beside the bricks were a plate, cutlery, a glass and an empty wine bottle."

"In that case, perhaps she thought it might warm the tent up," reasoned Debbie, "although I doubt it and can't see why as it was far from chilly last night. In fact Gideon commented on how muggy it was when he came home from choir practice."

"I suppose she might have been feeling cold or perhaps a little unwell," said Hetty, "but as you say, I doubt it. What's more, surely a woman of forty-five or whatever age she is or was, would know about carbon monoxide poisoning, especially being a mystery crime writer."

Kitty licked her finger and picked up pieces of grated cheese that had fallen from her sandwich onto her plate, "I'm inclined to agree with you, Het. It doesn't look like an accident to me."

"So," mused Debbie, "all indications point to suicide."

"Actually, we're jumping the gun a bit by assuming carbon monoxide poison was the cause of death," said Lottie, "it could have been something completely different."

"Good point, so we'll have to wait for the post mortem results." Kitty having cleared her plate reached for a slice of cake.

"I don't think they'll pass the results on to us, Kit," chuckled Hetty. "Be nice if they did though."

"Oh, Het, you know what I mean. Anyway, once the results are known it'll become common knowledge soon enough, especially when Tess gets to hear."

Later that same day, inside the police station, Detective Inspector David Bray weighed up the evidence in the case of Beatrice Cookson. Without doubt Mrs Cookson's death was caused by hemlock poisoning, leaves of which may have been placed or dropped onto her salad inside the Crown and Anchor. According to her cousin, Shelley Sinclair, she had given some of her salad and the dressing to Mrs Cookson because the dressing was not to her liking. There were, however, no witnesses to this manoeuvre. CCTV did not cover the table in question and because the plates were washed long before Mrs Cookson was found dead there was no forensic evidence that the salad was where the hemlock leaves were hidden. However, any suggestion of the poisoning having occurred earlier in the day was out of the question, for according to a toxicology report, an adult who had ingested a sufficient dose of hemlock for it to be fatal would show narcotic-like effects as soon as thirty minutes after ingestion, with the victim falling asleep and into unconsciousness until death followed a few hours later.

Leaving the cause of death to one side, there was also a motive to consider. No-one it appears benefitted from Mrs Cookson's death and her husband was certainly not involved because he had rock solid alibis for the day and evening before his wife's death. And now Shelley Sinclair herself was dead and preliminary investigations seemed to indicate that she had taken her own life. According to Mrs Dale, landlady of the Crown and Anchor, Ms Sinclair had been feeling low the evening before she was found dead and intended to drown her sorrows in a bottle of wine. Did she do so because of grief or was it possible she ended her life overcome with guilt because she had poisoned Beatrice Cookson herself? But if the latter were the case, why? Was it possible that Ms Sinclair being a writer of crime fiction wanted to witness the process of someone's demise through hemlock poisoning to enable her to write an accurate account? Possible, yes, but there was no evidence to back that theory up and were she to have used that method of murder in a subsequent book she would have given herself away.

Tess had just begun her evening shift at the Crown and Anchor when a couple she had not seen before entered the bar from the little used front door out onto the street. Not that it was that unusual to encounter strangers. Being a coastal village there were always a lot of unfamiliar faces around, but for some unknown reason Tess's heart went out to the couple taking in their surroundings as they slowly approached the bar. Perhaps it was because they reminded her of her late parents or perhaps it was because even though they were in the autumn of their years they stuck close together like a pair of newly-weds.

Tess being Tess put them at ease by welcoming them and introducing herself. In return they told her their names were Mary and Joseph Baker and they were staying at Sea View Cottage until Bank Holiday Monday. Furthermore, during their stay they would be looking at property as they were thinking of leaving their Surrey home now Joseph had retired and spending the rest of their lives in Cornwall. Tess on hearing their names, Mary and Joseph, was intrigued, whereupon they told her that when they first met and told each other their names, both knew they were meant for each other and they had been together for fifty years.

After looking warily over her shoulder, Mary asked, "Is it true, dear, that someone was murdered here the other day?"

"Sadly yes. It was a lady staying on our campsite. She was poisoned with hemlock and the police are treating it as murder but there's always the chance it was an accident so please don't let it worry you." Tess, relieved the couple had entered the pub by the front door and not the side car park entrance from which they would have seen the police investigating a second death, prayed they would ask no more questions. To change the subject she pointed to the poster on the notice board advertising the church fete.

"Yes, we know about that," said Joseph, "we went to church yesterday morning as it's just over the road from our cottage and the vicar, such a nice young man, mentioned it during the service."

As Mary and Joseph sipped their drinks out on the sun terrace overlooking the beach, Harry, Jake and Jack returned from a day out kayaking and found that the police had sealed off the field. Shortly after, the four girls returned from a look around Marazion, along with other campers who had been out for the day. The police officer preventing access to the field briefly explained what had happened and told the campers they would be allowed to return after seven o'clock. Several stayed to observe the police procedure while others went into the pub considering it the best place to find out more.

At seven-thirty, when they were allowed to return to their temporary accommodation, Jake pointed to the disposable barbecue beneath their caravan. "Hard to think something as innocent looking as a throwaway barbecue can be a killer."

"I think we ought to get rid of it. Just seeing it gives me the creeps," said Jack.

Harry nodded," Yeah, we'll do that." But as he bent to pick it up, he paused.

"What's wrong?" Jake asked.

"Did either of you move it after we'd finished with it last night?" Harry looked puzzled.

"Nope," said Jack, "You were the last to touch it. You said you were bringing it over here in case someone tripped over it on the path by the picnic table."

"Exactly, but I didn't leave it under the caravan. I put it under the steps on the gravel because it was still red-hot. So hot in fact I had to grab a tea towel so I could pick it up. What's more, it's now full of water."

Jake laughed. "That's because it rained last night, you numpty. It was a right racket and woke me up."

"Yes, but the rain wouldn't have got under the caravan, would it?"

Jack looked worried. "You reckon someone moved it then?"

"Yeah. And tipped water in it?"

"But why?"

"I don't know." Harry gripped the arms of his two friends, "Don't touch it because something's not right. I'm going in the pub to tell Dad."

Chapter Fifteen

The following morning, Emma, with a day off work, having done her share of the housework, decided to go down to the beach for a swim. As she walked across the sand she heard someone call her name. Sitting on a towel waving her hand was Suzy, one of the wigwam girls. Happy to see a familiar face, Emma went to join her.

"I'm so glad you're here," gushed Suzy, "I feel really self-conscious sitting on my own. You know, like I have no friends."

"But you do have friends," Emma glanced across the beach, "although I can't see them."

"That's because they've gone to the Scilly Isles for the day. They wanted me to go too but I said no way. They've gone by helicopter, you see and I'm terrified of heights."

"But it's only a short flight. Fifteen minutes or so."

"Yes, that's what they said but that'd seem like fifteen hours to me."

"Shame. I've been there a couple of times and it's really pretty. Lots of places to walk and the air is really fresh."

"That's why they wanted to go. They liked the idea of there being little or no traffic. Anyway, please sit down. I'd like to hear more of your wedding details."

"Of course."

Emma sat and after describing the dresses of herself and the bridesmaids, the flowers and where they were going for their honeymoon, she asked Suzy if she had a boyfriend."

"No I don't but I really like Dee and wish he lived back home so I could get to know him."

"Dee?"

"Yes, you know. He plays guitar with Treacle Toffee."

"Of course. Silly me. I should know, he lives next door to Zac's Grandma and Great Auntie Het. Nice bloke. Works in the Pasty shop. His real name is Derek but he hates it and that's why he calls himself Dee but don't tell him I told you that."

"I won't. So how old is he?"

"Nineteen, I think. How old are you?"

Suzy groaned. "Twenty, so that means I'm older than him."

"So what? I'm a year or so older than Zac and it makes no difference."

"No, I suppose not. Anyway, to change the subject, what do you think about the two ladies that died? Gretel reckons Shelley poisoned her cousin and then committed suicide because she felt guilty."

"That seems to be what most people are saying but I don't know, I reckon there's more to it than that. Not that I knew either of the ladies. In fact I never even got to speak to them."

"I did and they were both really, really nice. Especially Shelley, she often commented on our keep fit routine even though I think she thought we were bonkers."

As Emma was about to reply, Claude Dexter crossed the beach nearby with a newspaper tucked beneath his arm. On seeing Emma he waved and she waved back.

"Isn't he the bloke married to the MP?" Suzy asked.

"That's right and I know him because he's a friend of the Liddicott-Treens, my bosses at Pentrillick House. Although I hadn't met him or his wife until they arrived a week or so ago to judge the Pentrillick in Bloom competition." Emma watched as Claude sat down on one of the benches and unfolded his newspaper.

"I thought it was him." Suzy chuckled, "Shelley told us that he told her he was familiar with the novels she wrote. I think he must have been pulling her leg. I mean, he doesn't look the type to read romantic murder mysteries, does he?"

"No, I suppose not."

"My grandparents might know more about him but I doubt it. They live a couple of streets away from him in the constituency where his wife is the Member of Parliament, you see."

"Really! And did they vote for her in the last election?"

"Granddad did and he thinks she's wonderful. Grandma on the other hand dislikes her intensely and so needless to say, didn't. Politics is something to be avoided when we visit them."

"Very wise."

Inside his office, DI David Bray who along with other members of his team had initially assumed Shelley's death was either accidental due to lack of awareness regarding carbon monoxide or suicide, were interested to hear what Harry Dale had to say. Consequently the boys' barbecue was taken away for forensic examination. To the surprise of all they found none of the boys' fingerprints on their aluminium foil tray, but Shelley Sinclair's were. Likewise, on the barbecue found in the deceased's tent, the boys' fingerprints were evident but Shelley Sinclair's were not. This piece of information brought up another and more likely scenario. Shelley Sinclair was murdered. Furthermore, it was possible that Shelley was the intended victim for the first murder and not her cousin, Beatrice. With two likely murders to investigate the police returned to the Crown and Anchor to question staff and campers further.

Hetty and Lottie, on duty in the charity shop, were just about to close up for the day when Tess came in to relay the latest news. Jackie, who had worked the eleven til four shift in the pub and been questioned by the police, had phoned Tess after leaving work to put her in the picture.

Both sisters were shocked.

"This attack on Shelley must be linked to the death of Beatrice then," reasoned Hetty.

Lottie nodded. "I agree and it looks as though Shelley might have been the intended victim in the first instance and the killer somehow got their plates muddled up."

Tess shook her head. "No, that wouldn't be the case because if you remember Shelley said she gave most of her salad to Beatrice because she didn't like the spicy dressing. Meaning the hemlock may well have been on Shelley's plate and she removed it when she passed her salad to Beatrice."

"Must be the case then, so now we need to find a motive for someone to kill Shelley if Beatrice's death was an accident."

"But then again Beatrice might have picked up the hemlock somewhere else," said Lottie, "I mean, if it only takes a small quantity to kill someone it could have been in anything. Remember, Shelley believed Beatrice had lunch somewhere in town so she might simply have bought a ready-made supermarket sandwich."

"Well if that's the case then neither of the cousins would have been targeted as the sandwich or whatever would have been made by a worker who probably bore a grudge against his or her employer," reasoned Hetty, "Having said that, I wonder how long after hemlock's eaten, it becomes fatal?"

"Good point," agreed Lottie, "It's something we ought to look into."

Tess groaned. "Well the best of luck because to me the possibilities seem endless."

"Yes," agreed Hetty, "but I think we'll assume Shelley was the target in both cases and after we've done a bit of research into hemlock we'll concentrate on motives and let the police deal with the rest."

"That's very generous of you," laughed Tess, "I'm sure the police will be delighted to know that."

Hetty tutted. "Well, you know what I mean."

"Of course and the best of luck."

Lottie wasn't so sure. "On the other hand, I really think we ought to keep an open mind on the off chance each cousin was the intended victim in each case and that someone bore a grudge against them both for some reason or other."

Tess smiled. "I'll have to leave you to it as I'm due at work in ten minutes. Let me know if you get anywhere, won't you?"

"Of course, and thanks for keeping us up to date."

"My pleasure."

As Tess left, Lottie dropped the catch on the door behind her and turned the OPEN notice to CLOSED. They then cashed up, gathered their belongings and left the shop, eager to get home and mull over information received.

Chapter Sixteen

"Let's look at Beatrice first," said Hetty, as they sat down with fish and chips bought on their way home as neither was in the mood to cook. "Who will have benefitted from her demise?"

Lottie picked up the vinegar and shook it liberally over her food. "Her husband might, I suppose. Assuming they owned their house."

"Yes, that's the trouble. We don't know anything about him and the only person who would have known is also dead. It's so frustrating."

"The same goes for Shelley. I mean, we do know that she wasn't married and had no descendants but we've no idea whether or not she'd written a will and even if she had we're not likely to find out who'll benefit."

"And if we did have a name it's unlikely it'd mean anything. Although I'm sure she said something about a brother. Yes, she did. She said she bought him out when they inherited their parents' house. Can't remember his name though."

"I wonder. Might it be worth looking on Facebook, Het? Remember, Shelley granted you a friend request when we first met her so you'll be able to see her contacts."

"Well done, Lottie. Yes, that is a good idea and I'll look up Beatrice while I'm at it. If she is on Facebook then the chances are her husband will be too and if so I'll send him our condolences and explain briefly who we are."

Hetty placed her knife and fork on her plate and logged into her Facebook account. She viewed Shelley's friends and as anticipated Beatrice was there along with her husband Brian. On his page were several messages of condolences. "Right, I won't do it now because I want to finish my dinner and I need to think out what to say anyway, but when I've thought it through, I'll send Brian a private message."

"Good idea, but let me know what you've written before you send it to get a second opinion."

"Will do."

While Lottie washed up, Hetty wrote a short message and read it to Lottie when she returned to the living room with two mugs of tea.

It read:

Dear Brian, You don't know me, but I live in Cornwall at Pentrillick and while they were here, my friends and I had the good fortune to meet your wife, Beatrice, and her cousin, Shelley Sinclair. We shared a few precious moments together and learned a little of their lives - your lives.

I, my friends and everyone in the village are deeply saddened and shocked by the deaths of the two ladies. Please accept our deepest condolences.

With love and best wishes to you, your son, Marc, and other family members.

Henrietta Tonkins (Hetty).x

"Lovely," said Lottie with approval, "Let's hope it bears fruit."

After drinking their tea they Googled hemlock and concluded, as had the police, that Beatrice must have ingested the leaves in the evening at the Crown and Anchor. For had it been earlier at lunchtime, symptoms would have been evident long before she had returned from her trip to Penzance.

The following afternoon, much to Hetty's surprise, she received a reply to her message of condolence.

It read:

Thank you Hetty for your kind words. It's been hard for us to make sense of what's happened but Marc and me are finally accepting that our beloved Beatrice is gone forever. I've spoken to Shell's brother, Steve, who is equally gutted. We neither of us can think who'd want to hurt the girls. Beat and Shell were loved by many. We can't think of a motive either. Me and Beat owned our place between us and no-one else will benefit from her will. Likewise, Shell's place will go to her brother Steve's boy.

Thank you again for your good wishes. In the few text messages I had from Beat she said what a lovely place Pentrillick is. I'm glad she was happy for the last days of her life.

Regards, Brian and Marc.

Eager to show the messages to Debbie and Kitty, Hetty rang them and the four agreed to meet up in the Crown and Anchor that evening.

When the ladies arrived at the pub, Lottie observed that Shelley's tent had been removed and flowers lay in its place. Out of curiosity they crossed the field to take a closer look. Standing on bricks was a glass jar full of water and a bouquet of flowers with a note saying, *Sleep tight dear ladies. Love from the wigwam girls. xx.* Around it other people had also laid their contributions.

"We must do the same," said Debbie.

Hetty agreed. "We'll pick some flowers in the morning and drop them here on our way to work."

Inside the pub, the ladies took seats around their favourite table and after drinks were purchased Hetty read out the messages between herself and Beatrice's husband, Brian.

"So let's see if I've got this right," said Debbie as the words sank in, "No-one benefits financially from Beatrice's death but the son of Shelley's brother Steve will inherit Shelley's estate."

"Correct," said Hetty.

Debbie leaned back in her chair. "Then surely he must be our number one suspect."

"That's what we think," said Lottie, "but how do we go about finding out. I mean, we don't even know his name."

"Well his surname must be Sinclair," reasoned Kitty, "Shelley never married so her name would be the same as her brother, Steve."

"True," agreed Hetty, "but some authors have pen-names so she might not be a Sinclair at all."

Kitty tutted. "Damn, you're right."

"How about going on Facebook and looking through Shelley's friends. If he's her nephew he might be amongst them."

Acknowledging it was worth a try, Hetty scrolled through Shelley's friends. "Aha, this could be him. He's called Jack and looks to be in his early twenties."

"Right age then," agreed Lottie.

Hetty scrolled down his posts. "Bingo. It was his birthday back in May and here's a message from Auntie Shell wishing him a happy birthday."

"Jack," Debbie gasped. "Could he be the same Jack who is friends with Harry?"

Hetty looked horrified. "Goodness me. I hope not."

"Is there a picture of him?" Kitty asked.

"Yes, but it's not very good because he's in fancy dress. All I can be sure of is he has dark hair." Hetty passed her phone around the table.

"Hmm, can't say that he looks familiar," said Lottie, "Having said that I know that Harry's mates are called Jack and Jake because Kate and Vicki have made friends with them and although I've seen them briefly, I've no idea which is which and neither of them look much like Shelley's nephew anyway."

"This is silly," said Kitty, "because if he was Shelley's nephew he'd be upset and with Shelley and Beatrice being cousins he'd be related to them both."

"He'd not be upset if he was responsible for their deaths," reasoned Hetty.

Lottie glanced around the bar to see if Harry and his friends were in and to her relief there was no sign of them. "I'm inclined to agree with Kitty," she said, "and on top of that is the fact that there would have been no need for this Jack person to poison Beatrice if it was Shelley's estate he was after."

"I agree even though we're pretty sure Beatrice's death was accidental," said Debbie, "What's more, I think because we don't have a clue about anything we're just grasping at straws. I mean, if Harry's friend, Jack is Shelley's nephew, then the police will have established that by now and checked him out."

"Humph, well, we'll see and I suggest we keep an open mind," Hetty switched off her phone. "I wonder, do either of you have a tent?"

Looking puzzled, Kitty and Debbie both shook their heads.

"Why on earth do you ask that?" spluttered Lottie. "Surely you aren't thinking of going camping, Het."

"Why not? A night camping on the pub field might throw up a few clues. After all, I think you'll agree that the person or persons behind the two deaths is most likely one of the campers even if Harry's friend Jack isn't the right Jack and it isn't a Jack we're after anyway."

"The pub field!" Lottie looked aghast. "Surely you're not thinking of camping there!"

"Yes. Why not?"

"You can't do that when we only live up the road. You'd look daft and goodness only knows what James and Ella would think."

Debbie smothered a smile. "Anyway, Het, the police will already have looked into the campers and I know for a fact that they've all been questioned and have made statements."

"And no doubt they'll all have alibis for the two nights in question," said Lottie. "What's more, any Tom, Dick or Harry could have put poison in the salad or have put the barbecue in Shelley's tent. It wouldn't have to be a camper. Anyone leaving the pub or just passing by could have done it."

"No, whoever sneaked the hemlock on the plate must have been inside the pub," said Hetty, in defence. "Furthermore, whoever did the barbecue swap must have been on the field to know the lads had a midnight feast in the first place. So it has to be a camper."

"No, it doesn't," said Debbie, "anyone leaving the pub could have seen the lads barbecuing and crept back later."

"Okay, you win but we can't go camping anyway without a tent."

"Talking of tents," said Lottie, "Where do you think Shelley and Beatrice's tent is now?"

"I suppose the police took it away," reasoned Debbie, "they probably want to give it and its contents a thorough testing or whatever."

"That's a good point," mused Hetty, all thoughts of camping having gone from her mind, "Because if that is the case then surely it means that once the police have finished with it, someone, either Brian or Steve, will come down to collect it and its contents. That could help us greatly."

"Help us greatly," repeated Kitty, "In what way?"

109

"By giving us the chance to meet them and ask a few questions, of course."

"But surely they'll collect the stuff from the police station, Het," reasoned Debbie, "So how will we see them?"

"Well we could...."

"...No," snapped Lottie, "We're not sitting outside the police station for days on end hoping to spot them. We'd most likely get arrested."

"And we don't know what either Brian or Steve look like," Debbie added.

Hetty was downcast and then her face brightened. "We do. Their pictures are on their Facebook pages. What's more one of them might just mention coming down here so we'd know when to keep a look out."

"Maybe but we wouldn't know which police station, would we?"

"There can't be that many, surely," Hetty took out her phone again and Googled police stations in West Cornwall, "Well according to this there are several but I think the most likely would be Camborne, Helston or Truro. Or even Falmouth, I suppose."

"That's four," gasped Lottie, "We can't watch all four."

"We could if we split up."

"But you and I only have one car between us, Het."

"True but then I don't think we need to cover all four. Maybe just do two and we'll go in pairs."

Debbie decided to humour Hetty. "Okay then, we'll do as you say but only if we know for sure that Steve or Brian are coming down here, and when."

Chapter Seventeen

After several damp and drizzly days, the following morning dawned bright and sunny, and while Hetty prepared breakfast, Lottie went into the garden to gather flowers. She made up a colourful bouquet of dahlias and cosmos and for greenery added pittosporum. To extend their life, she placed the flowers in a plastic bottle and filled it with water. On their way to work at the charity shop the sisters placed their offering amongst others, keeping the bottle upright with a label attached saying *RIP Shelley & Beatrice, love from Debs, Kit, Lottie & Het.* As they were about to leave, one of Harry's friends emerged from the static caravan. Curious to know if he was Jake or Jack, the sisters considered how best to find out. However, a plan was not necessary for as the person in question stepped onto the grass, Harry opened the caravan door and called out: "Actually rather than a doughnut get me a chocolate éclair please, Jack."

"That answers that question then," said Lottie, as they left the field. "Harry's Jack is blond and looks nothing like Steve's son, Jack who has dark hair and I must say it's a great relief."

Hetty agreed, for although she had thought him a possible suspect, his link with the Dales would have made the situation very unpleasant.

Later, as the sisters sorted through donations in the charity shop, Hetty paused, something clearly on her mind. "It's just a thought, but I wonder if Shelley was murdered by someone who felt besmirched by the fact she had based a character in one of her novels on said person and everyone knew to whom she was referring. If you see what I mean."

"It's an interesting theory," Lottie acknowledged, "but if that is the case we've no way of finding out because we're not familiar with her work."

"But we would be if we read some of her books."

"Yes, I suppose we could do that. How many did Debbie say she had written?"

"Seventeen I think."

"And Debbie's already read one. So if we read one or two more between us it might give us some idea. After all, we only need descriptions of the villains. No-one would take umbrage if a goody was based on them, would they?"

"Exactly. One problem though," said Hetty, "We don't have any copies of her books and my Kindle has been out of action since I dropped it in the pond. I suppose I could buy another but that would take a day or two."

Lottie chuckled. "We'll have to buy paperbacks on-line then even though that'll take a day or two as well. And it won't be money down the drain because we both like reading anyway. Then when we've finished with them we can put them in the bookcase here. We know she has a fan in Clara."

However, the purchase of books on-line was not necessary because in the afternoon, as luck would have it, Pickle the gardener, popped into the shop with several copies of Shelley's earlier works. "I thought you might like these," he said. "I've had 'em for ages, well several years anyway, and I thought you know, after what happened to the poor woman they might be of interest and sell well."

"Collectors' items even," smiled Hetty.

Lottie took the books and looked at the covers. "I assume you've read them all."

Pickle pulled a face. "Not likely. Well actually out of curiosity I did read one but I didn't think much of it. Too much romance and soppy women's stuff. I like a bit of blood and thunder."

"So why did you buy more than one?" Hetty was confused.

"Because I bought them and a load of others, blind. I was at a car boot sale, you see, and one of the sellers had loads and loads of books for sale. He said he was having a clear out and needed to get rid of some, so had boxed them up in batches of twenty and was selling them for three pounds a box. It wasn't possible to see what was in them but I bought a box anyway and these were amongst them."

"I see," said Lottie, "well thank you very much. I'm sure they'll be appreciated."

When the sisters arrived back at Primrose Cottage they rang Debbie and then Kitty and told them about Pickle's donations and the fact they each had a book to read that evening. Intrigued by their theory as to who might have taken Shelley's life, Debbie and Kitty collected a book each and they all agreed to chew over the facts the next day.

The four ladies spent Friday evening and several hours on Saturday morning reading in order to finish their assigned books before lunch, for in the afternoon all were to help out at the church fete.

In 2020 and 2021, church members had agreed to give the fete a miss because of the pandemic. Prior to that, for many years, the fetes were held on the pub field, but since James and Ella had taken over the Crown and Anchor and opened up the field for campers there was no longer sufficient room during the church's chosen month of August. Consequently the owners of the care home offered the church use of their gardens and grounds which ran beyond the care home towards open fields. They also offered them access to their kitchen and toilets.

The morning of Saturday was dull with threatening grey clouds but by the lunchtime the clouds had dispersed and the sun was out. Ideal conditions, for the organisers knew from past experience that if the weather was too hot and sunny they would lose potential patrons to the beach.

Hetty and Lottie had agreed to help by running the teas and refreshment tent. Debbie had opted for plants and garden produce along with her husband, Gideon. And Kitty, with a stall displaying a vast array of prizes was prepared to sell raffle tickets along with Tess.

"I hope we're really busy and the time whizzes by," said Hetty, as she tipped a bucket of water from the care home kitchen into the tea urn, "because I'm longing to hear what Debbie and Kitty thought of Shelley's books."

"Me too," agreed Lottie, "but I also hope we're busy to make lots of money. The church funds are rather low after two years with no fund raising events."

"Well yes, of course I hope we make lots of money too."

"Good afternoon ladies." The sisters turned round to see Vicar Sam in the tent's doorway, "I must say these cakes look rather tempting." He handed over a bag of change, "Your float."

"Ideal, thank you," Lottie tipped the cash into an empty biscuit tin.

The fete was opened at two o' clock by guest speaker, Simone Dexter MP. Present were a large group of people who had flooded into the grounds when the care home gates were unfastened just minutes before. On hearing the words, '*I declare this fete open*,' patrons clapped and then dashed around hoping to find a bargain or two on the many well-stocked stalls.

Inside the tea tent, Hetty and Lottie were overwhelmed by customers. Seeing they looked slightly harassed, holidaymaker Mary, staying at Sea View Cottage, who had just entered the tent with Joseph, told her husband she would help the ladies for a while and suggested he made himself useful somewhere too. The sisters, who until then had seen Mary and Joseph but had no reason to speak to them, were very grateful for Mary's help despite the fact she seemed eager to take control.

Meanwhile, to while away the time, Joseph, who had an interest in gardening, made a bee-line for the plants and garden produce stall where Percy Pickering, also a keen gardener, was browsing the colourful display of flowers and vegetables. To his delight, Percy had found two named fuchsia varieties he didn't have to add to his already substantial collection.

"Good choice, Pickle. These are from cuttings I took from my own plants and I guarantee that they'll both flower well." Gideon took the five pound note proffered and handed Pickle two pounds change.

"Are you the chap who played the organ in church on Sunday?" Joseph asked Gideon.

"Yes, I am. Kitty Thomas and I take it in turns to do the morning and evening services."

"I thought so. I never forget a face, you see. Lovely church by the way, and lovely vicar too. Mary and I thought his sermon was very interesting. We like the village as well. In fact we wouldn't mind settling down here."

"Yes, it's a very popular village. We've been here five years or so now and it's the best move we've ever made."

Pickle chuckled, "I've been here all my life. Pentrillick born and bred." Having placed the plants carefully in a bag, he then said goodbye to Gideon and Debbie, nodded towards Joseph, and continued to walk around the grounds to see if anything else took his fancy. From the jumble stall he bought a fleece jacket which he carefully placed around the plants for added protection. He then bought raffle tickets, had a go on the tombola and finally popped in the refreshment tent for a cup of tea, a sandwich and a current bun. Feeling replenished and keen to get home away from the noise of piped music, screaming children and barking dogs, he crossed the lawn to the car park where he had left his bicycle leaning against a privet hedge. He tied the bag containing his purchases onto a rack behind the saddle, and after bidding farewell to Vicar Sam standing by the gate chatting to Sid, he set off down the lane towards the village. As he neared the bottom of the hill he pulled on the brakes to slow himself down. Nothing happened. He tried and failed again as the bicycle gathered speed. Cursing beneath his breath, he once more pulled hard on the brake levers and then shouted in frustration as the bicycle ran across the junction and into the main road. Luckily the road was clear in both directions as he flew across the tarmac, hit the kerb opposite with force, and flipped over the handlebars into a granite gatepost, whence he fell backwards into a ditch. The last thing Pickle heard before he lost consciousness was the sound of music drifting down the hill from the fete.

Meanwhile, Sid, who had promised to help Dolly in the pasty shop at half past three so that Eve could leave early because she and boyfriend Jude were going away for the weekend, concluded his chat with the vicar and set off down the hill. As he reached the bottom he saw a car had pulled up on the side of the road opposite and its driver was on his mobile phone. Sensing something was wrong, he quickened his pace. As he crossed the road he saw Pickle's bicycle, its wheels still spinning and Pickle lying apparently lifeless underneath.

"Ambulance and police are on their way." The car driver returned the phone to his pocket: "I've checked for a pulse and he's alive, thank God."

"Did you see what happened?" Sid stooped down, leaned over Pickle and touched his cheek, he then looked at the bicycle.

"No, but the police said not to touch anything."

"No, I won't but look at the bike." Sid pointed to the front brake cable: "that either snapped on impact or it's been cut deliberately."

The driver knelt down beside him. "Good heavens! It must have been deliberate because look, the back cable is severed too."

In the evening, Hetty and Lottie met up with Kitty and Debbie at the Crown and Anchor, not only to air their views on Shelley Sinclair's books but to discuss Pickle's accident also. For news of the gardener's misfortune had quickly made its way back to the fete leaving patrons and stall holders alike speculating as to what might have happened.

"Let's look at Pickle first," said Hetty, as they took their seats. "Does anyone know how he is?" All shook their heads. "Then we'd better find out." She took her purse from her handbag, "I'll get the drinks and ask at the bar. It happened not far from here so hopefully they'll be in the know."

Hetty returned shortly after with four glasses of red wine on a tray. "I've spoken to James and he says Pickle's injuries are not life threatening. He has a couple of broken ribs, he's sprained his wrist and has concussion. They're keeping him in overnight and will see how he is in the morning."

"Well, that's something," said Debbie, "Poor chap, he bought a couple of fuchsias from our stall at the fete. He was ever so pleased with them but they no doubt got crushed when he fell in the ditch."

"Is it true the brake cables were cut?" Kitty asked. "Dolly said Sid reckoned they were. I saw her just as I was coming down here, you see, and she said poor Sid was in a right state when he arrived at the pasty shop and kept apologising to Eve for delaying her getting off early. Oh yes, and before I forget, I don't know whether or not you've heard but the fete did really well and made just over one thousand pounds profit. I rang Vicar Sam to ask, you see, and needless to say he's delighted."

117

"That's brilliant. I know we were mega busy in the tea tent, in fact had Mary whatever she's called not come to our rescue, we wouldn't have coped." Hetty glanced around the bar to see if Mary was in with Joseph so that she could thank her again but it appeared she was not.

"That's good news," said Lottie, "but going back to Pickle, if his brake cables were cut it must have been deliberate but who on earth would want to hurt a harmless chap like him?"

"No idea, but I daresay we'll find out in due course. That's if the police find anything to go on, which I doubt." Having placed the glasses of wine on the table, Hetty sat down and leaned the tray against the legs of her chair.

"I agree," said Lottie, "anyway, shall we change the subject and get on to Shelley's books?"

"Humph! Rather a lot of extramarital affairs," was Debbie's first comment, "Seems like she had a thing for married men."

Hetty nodded her head. "We both said exactly the same, didn't we, Lottie?"

"Yes, we did and I found it quite nauseating."

"Likewise," agreed Kitty.

Debbie took a sip of her wine. "Well, if we're all in agreement I think it's safe to assume that the reason a person took Shelley's life was most likely in revenge for a possible marriage break-up rather than because she had based a character on him or her and thus besmirched their character."

Kitty wasn't convinced. "A bit extreme though, don't you think?"

"It depends how bad the break-up was," said Lottie, impressed with Debbie's line of thinking. "Some result in homelessness, poverty and not to mention loss of face."

"But surely in a marriage break-up the wife usually comes out alright," reasoned Hetty, "and as far as we know Shelley never actually stole anyone's husband. Not to

118

marry him anyway because she was emphatic that she was single and liked it that way."

"That's a good point. I hadn't considered that." Debbie took another sip of her wine. "Changing the subject slightly: unless there's something wrong with my taste buds this isn't the usual wine, is it, Het?"

"No, James said they couldn't get their usual so had to go for this instead but I think it's rather nice."

"Nice, I think it's delicious. Very fruity."

"Richer too," agreed Lottie, "and to tell you the truth, I think I prefer it."

"Me too," agreed Kitty, "in fact if you drink up ladies I'll get us all refills." Kitty drained her glass and reached for the empty tray.

"And while you're at the bar, tell James we all prefer it," said Hetty, "he said to let him know what we thought."

After Kitty returned with their refills they attempted to resume their scrutiny of the two murder cases.

"Where were we?" Hetty asked.

"We were trying to fathom out if Shelley might have caused the marriage break-up of someone or other and given them cause to wish her harm and take revenge," Kitty reminded her.

"That's right," said Debbie, "and I still think it's worth pursuing. I mean, with a lot of women humiliation alone would be enough for them to seek revenge, especially if the man they've lost, even on a temporary basis, was a prominent figure."

"True," Lottie agreed.

"But how do we go about finding suspects?" Debbie asked. "There have been loads of people here on holiday this summer and there still are a lot about but I never heard anybody mention Shelley except during the days following her death when everyone was talking about her."

"We could always ask the crystal ball to help," suggested Hetty.

119

Lottie tutted. "Now you're being silly, Het."

"I think it's this wine. Anyone for another?" Hetty stood up.

All drained their glasses: even Kitty who usually stopped at two.

An hour later having made no progress with their sleuthing and having decided to sleep on their thoughts, the four ladies gathered together their belongings ready to go to their respective homes. As they stood, MP Simone Dexter, leaving the pub with her husband Claude, paused by their table. "I've been watching you," she said, po-faced," and you drink far too much for ladies of your age."

Hetty opened her mouth to respond in defence but could think of nothing to say."

Claude meanwhile, behind his wife's back, winked at the ladies and slapped his wrist in mock reprimand thus causing Debbie to giggle.

Simone Dexter, not amused, haughtily tossed her head and left with Claude following behind.

"What a cheek," burbled Kitty.

"Absolutely," agreed Hetty, "ladies of our age indeed! That's racist."

"I think you mean ageist," chuckled Debbie.

"Well, whatever."

"She has a point though, Het," said Lottie, "and I think someone said that to us once before. What's more, I've a feeling we won't be up in time for church at nine tomorrow."

"Church," Kitty groaned. "Thank goodness it's your Gideon's turn to play the organ in the morning, Debs."

Chapter Eighteen

"I'm just popping down to Saltwater House," said Lottie on Sunday morning, as she slipped her arms into her lightweight jacket. "Layton just rang and he sounds in a right pickle because he's dropped some stitches and can't work out what to do. He didn't want to confess at first but finally admitted restoration work is beyond his capabilities."

"Okay," Hetty, at the sink washing the breakfast dishes looked over her shoulder, "and while you've gone I'll make the Victoria Sandwich for this evening."

"I'll look forward to that especially if you use the fresh cream."

"I will, we've had it a couple of days now and I doubt we'll get round to making a trifle as planned."

"Should be delicious then especially if you use Kitty's homemade strawberry jam." Lottie picked up her bag and hung it on her shoulder, "I'll leave you to it but I won't be long."

"And take your brolly," called Hetty, as she heard Lottie open the front door, "it looks like it might be drizzling though I doubt it'll be much."

"Will do, bye."

After drying up, Hetty made the cake and to pass the time while the sandwich tins were in the oven, she sat down at the piano in the dining room and played some of her favourite tunes.

Meanwhile, walking up the hill was Paul Fox carrying a scarf she had left in the pub the previous evening. When he heard the sound of music drifting through the open dining room window, he paused to listen for several minutes before knocking on the door.

"Was it you playing the piano or was it Lottie?" He asked when Hetty answered the door.

"Me. Lottie's popped down to see Layton. Why?"

"Because it was beautiful and you were playing my favourite tune."

"Was I? Oh, that's nice to know." She opened the door wide. "Are you coming in?"

"If I may, yes. I'm here to bring back your scarf. You left it in the pub and Jackie spotted it after you'd gone. I said I'd drop it off this morning in case you wondered where it was."

"That's very kind but as it is, I hadn't even missed it." She frowned, "I don't remember seeing you in the pub last night."

"I came in quite late and ended up chatting with young Happy Harper about music." Paul stepped into the hallway and stooped to stroke Albert who having recognised the voice seemed eager to greet him. "I saw you and your mates in there but didn't bother you as you seemed deep in conversation. No doubt plotting something or other." He picked up Albert and closed the door behind him. "Something smells good."

Hetty ignored his ridicule regarding plotting. "It's only a cake. We're going down to the Old Bakehouse tonight, you see. Bill's making a curry because it's Jed's birthday and the cake is for afters."

"Very nice too."

After taking the cake layers from the oven, Hetty made two mugs of coffee while she waited for them to cool. They then went into the sitting room where Paul sat on the sofa with Albert on his lap.

"I think he likes you," said Hetty.

"And I like him too. In fact I'm seriously thinking about getting a dog now I've no commitments."

"Good idea. I highly recommend it."

"That's what Layton said. As you know he's devoted to George, and Clarence too of course."

"Yes, and while I think of it, is there any more news regarding poor old Pickle?"

"Not yet but hopefully we'll hear later when the doctors have done their rounds."

"And were the brake cables cut or did they snap when the bike hit the gatepost?"

"What makes you think they might have been cut?"

"Kitty said last night that it looked as if they were. She got that from Dolly who got it from Sid. Sid of course being there shortly after it happened and before the police and what have you arrived."

"I see, and at the moment I don't know any more than you. I think it's unlikely though. I mean, Pickle got to the fete okay and from Hawthorn Road too so he must have gone down Goose Lane which is quite steep and the brakes must have been working then. So if they were tampered with it would have been done at the fete and I really can't see anyone risking that with so many people around." He shrugged his shoulders, "and what could be the motive anyway?"

"True, and I hope you're right. We don't want any more jiggery-pokery."

After finishing his coffee, Paul rose and gently lowered Albert onto the floor. "Sorry mate but I have to go now."

The reason for his departure was that one of his daughters was due to Facetime at half past eleven, so he needed to get back home. As he left the house, Hetty hung the silk scarf he'd returned on the coat pegs in the hallway and then watched as he walked away towards Long Lane. She chuckled to herself as she closed the door. Never in her wildest dreams, when she and Lottie had first encountered the now retired detective inspector, would she have imagined him to become one of her dearest friends.

In the evening, as pre-arranged, Hetty and Lottie walked down to the Old Bakehouse for Jed's birthday with the Victoria sandwich in an old biscuit tin. Barbara and Jed were already there having gone direct from their trip to Mevagissey where they had stayed overnight.

To the delight of the sisters, twins Kate and Vicki were not working so they were able to question them about the pub's recent guests and in particular ladies on their own in the forty to fifty age bracket.

"There was a woman on her own recently but she's gone home now," said Kate "and I can't remember her name."

"The one that's gone home was called Brenda Webb," said Vicki, "but there's another lady on her own who's still there and she's called Zena something or other."

"I think it's Marshall," said Kate.

"Hmm, sounds familiar."

"So what can you tell us about them?" Hetty eagerly asked.

Vicki shrugged her shoulders. "Mrs Webb, Brenda, liked plaice and chips but didn't want tartare sauce or a slice of lemon with it. That's all I know."

"What sort of age?" Lottie asked.

"Older than Mum but not as old as you, Grandma," said Vicki, impishly.

"Cheeky girl," tutted Sandra.

"How about the other woman. Zena Marshall?" Hetty asked, "How old do you reckon she is?"

"Younger than Mrs Webb," said Kate, "and she's prettier too."

"Looks like you two will have to interrogate Tess, if you want answers to your questions," said Bill, tongue in cheek.

"Yes, she'll know," said Vicki, "Tess always gets to know the guests."

"Why on earth do you want to know about the pub's female guests, Auntie Het?" Barbara asked.

"Hmm, err…" Hetty couldn't think of an innocent response.

"It'll be to do with the deaths of the two ladies camping on the pub field," explained Bill, "Mum and Auntie Het will be hot on the case along with their chums, Debbie Elms and Kitty Thomas."

Jed groaned. "Well you be careful. We get folks like that back in the States and they can be a right pain in the um…nether regions."

On Monday morning, Hetty and Lottie left Primrose Cottage for the charity shop sheltering beneath umbrellas but neither uttered a word of complaint; the rain was welcome and it was good to see hints of green on lawns and water dripping from shrivelled leaves. Beneath her arm, Lottie clutched a plastic bag containing the Shelley Sinclair novels they had read. At the Old Bakehouse the previous day they had asked Sandra to tell Clara, the care home's cook, they had some of Shelley's books when next she saw her at work. Although with the author's demise, the sisters reasoned the novels may well no longer be wanted as book signing was out of the question.

"Before we do anything," said Hetty, shaking her umbrella and placing it behind the counter, "I'm going to see who the crystal ball thinks is behind the deaths of Shelley and Beatrice. I've been thinking about it all morning and I'm none the wiser."

"Don't be silly, Het. It's not even a real crystal ball. Not the sort used by mediums and what have you anyway."

"That's harsh. Poor ball."

Lottie turned the sign on the door from CLOSED to OPEN and then watched as her sister waved her hands over the glass ball; with eyes closed Hetty asked in a silly voice who is responsible for the deaths of the two cousins. When she opened her eyes and looked at the ball she squealed and jumped back in disbelief. "It's her, Lottie. The MP woman. I just saw her face as clear as day."

Lottie rolled her eyes, stepped forwards and looked into the ball. "Well I can't see anyone and certainly not Simone Dexter."

"Oh, well perhaps you're not gifted like me," Although said tongue in cheek, Hetty wondered if it really might be the case.

"Maybe not but I don't know why you're bothering. I thought it was the two women staying at the pub we were focusing on now. You know, Zena Marshall and Brenda something or other."

"Webb. Yes, you're right it is and we've yet to tell Debbie and Kitty about them, so if you agree I suggest we call a meeting for this evening and put them in the picture."

"Okay but if you do I won't be there. Remember, Layton is taking me out for dinner tonight."

"Oh bother, I'd forgotten that. It'll just have to be Debbie, Kitty and me then."

In the evening, it was just Hetty and Debbie who met up in the Crown and Anchor for Kitty was also unable to join them as she and her husband Tommy had other plans. As they sipped their first drinks, Hetty told Debbie how she had seen Simone Dexter's face in the crystal ball.

Debbie frowned. "But if we're trying to find someone whose marriage might have been wrecked by Shelley it can't be Simone because she is still married."

"That's just what Lottie said. That and in my case it being wishful thinking because I don't like the woman. She was married before Claude though but her husband died. Something like that."

"Oh, that is sad." Debbie cast her eyes around the bar. "So who are we looking out for tonight? On the phone you said something about women staying here on their own."

"That's right. Zena Marshall and Brenda Webb. According to Vikki and Kate they were both around when our ladies died and they were on their own. In fact Zena is still here but the other one, Brenda, has gone home now. We need to find out what we can about them and their marital status in particular."

"In other words, you want to know if either or both are divorced."

"Yes."

"Okay, drink up then. It's my round so I'll see what Tess has to say."

While Debbie was at the bar, Barbara and Jed emerged from the dining room. Seeing Hetty, they headed in her direction. "Mind if we join you," asked Barbara, taking a seat. "Only for a few minutes though. We're waiting for Bill and Sandra and then we're all going to Pentrillick House to meet the Liddicott-Treens and see the ballroom where the wedding reception is to be held."

"Very nice too. The Liddicott-Treens are both lovely as are their children."

Barbara glanced around the bar. "Are you on your own?"

"No, no, I'm here with Debbie while your mum's out with her fancy man."

"Layton?"

"Yes. Apparently they were chatting about food yesterday morning when she went to save his knitting and got onto dishes that were all the rage in the sixties and seventies when we were young. You know, things like Coq au vin, duck à l'orange, boeuf bourguignon and spaghetti Bolognese. That led onto Layton saying he'd discovered a little place that specialised in nostalgic dishes and he's taken her there tonight." Hetty hoped Debbie would be subtle when she saw they had company. However, when she returned with the drinks, Debbie was smiling but being diplomatic she sat down and made small talk with Barbara

127

and Jed about the wedding. Shortly after, Sandra and Bill arrived and the four left.

"Phew!" sighed Hetty, "thanks for not dropping us in it, Debs. Jed, like Paul, doesn't approve of people, and ladies in particular, helping them solve cases."

"I suppose they call it interfering."

"They do. Bloomin' cheek. Anyway, did you find anything out?"

"Yes, that's Zena Marshall over there," Debbie nodded in the direction of the table by the French doors.

"The woman reading the Pentrillick Gazette?" Hetty wanted to make sure she had the right person.

"Yes, that's her."

"Ah, I've noticed her before. She was at the fete on Saturday wearing a gorgeous short, strappy dress and I felt quite envious and wondered where she bought it."

"Yes, I saw her too and thought how nice she looked. She must have felt chilly though. I mean, the weather was okay on Saturday, but it wasn't really warm enough for something sleeveless. I'm back in my cardigans now things are back to normal."

"Same with me. Anyway, what did you learn from Tess?"

"Well, we can forget Brenda Webb because she didn't arrive until after Beatrice died and according to Tess she's still married. The reason she was on her own is because she'd been ill and wanted to spend a few days by the sea. Her husband couldn't come down with her because he couldn't get the time off work."

Hetty rested her elbow on the table and cupped her chin in her hand. "Fair enough. What about Zena Marshall?"

"Now she's more interesting. She arrived two days after Beatrice and Shelley turned up and is of course still here. What's more she lives in Kent and is divorced."

"Bingo," squealed Hetty, "she has to somehow be involved."

"Well, not necessarily but it's a start. I mean, there's hardly enough evidence to make her a genuine suspect and as far as we know she's done nothing other than be here at the right time."

"Hmm, and if she was guilty surely she'd have scarpered before now. I know I would have."

Debbie was surprised. "Would you though? I mean if you had it would have looked suspicious, especially if you left before the date you were due to leave."

"True I suppose, but then I expect the police will have interviewed her anyway."

"Yes, I believe, like the campers, they interviewed everyone staying here on the nights the two ladies died and some of the pub's clientele too."

"On the other hand, it's possible the police are treating her as a suspect," reasoned Hetty, "I mean, were that the case they'd not make it public knowledge."

"So how do we go about finding out more about this Zena Marshall?" Debbie glanced over to Zena's table and was surprised to see she had been joined by Happy Harper.

"I suppose we could get to know her and ask questions, though I'm not comfortable with that."

"Me neither, and if she's guilty she might smell a rat and then do a runner." Debbie's face lit up. "I suppose we could follow her."

"Follow her! Follow her where?"

"Oh, I don't know but she must go somewhere during the daytime."

"Perhaps she has friends in the area," pondered Hetty.

"Precisely, and if that's the case we might be able to get close enough to her and whoever she meets and eavesdrop on their conversation."

"I like it. Nothing like a bit of eavesdropping."

"I agree, and while we're on the subject of friends, look, Happy is on her table now and they're chatting away like lifelong chums."

Hetty glanced over her shoulder. "Perhaps they are old friends then. I mean, he could well come from the same area."

Debbie frowned. "It's just occurred to me, Het. Happy was here when Shelley died, but what about Beatrice? Was he here then?"

"Can't remember, perhaps you could…"

"…No, said Debbie, "I'm not asking Tess."

"Okay. I don't think there's any need anyway. Zena's our suspect and we must focus on her for now. The trouble with following her though is we don't know where she'll go. If she goes anywhere at all."

"Well she's hardly going to stay in her room all day long so we'll follow wherever she does go," said Debbie, "after all you don't work in the charity shop on Tuesdays so your day will be free."

Hetty nodded her head sagely. "Okay. The more I think about it the more I like the idea. I mean, not only might it be productive but it'll be a bit of fun as well."

"What's the weather forecast for tomorrow?"

Hetty looked at her phone. "Fine, dry with a bit of sun here and there."

"Ideal, we'll follow her tomorrow then although I'm not sure how to go about it?"

"It's simple," Hetty dropped her phone back into her bag, "we'll pop in here for a coffee when they open tomorrow at eleven and keep an eye on the door that leads to the guests' rooms."

"But she might have already gone out by then," reasoned Debbie.

"No, I doubt it. She's still here now and has a full glass of whatever so I should imagine she's not an early riser."

"What if she goes out in a car?"

Hetty clucked her tongue. "Good point. So we'll have to make sure we have a car down here just in case. No problem with parking as we can use the pub's car park if we're coming in here for a coffee. Meanwhile, I'll send Kitty a text and see if she'd like to come along too."

"And Lottie. She must join us."

Hetty chuckled. "I don't think Lottie will take much persuading."

"Me neither. Which reminds me, has there been any mention of either Shelley's brother or Beatrice's husband, coming down to pick up the tent and stuff?"

"Good gracious, how very remiss of me. Because we went to the Old Bakehouse last night, I haven't checked since yesterday morning." Hetty again pulled her phone from her handbag and quickly logged into Facebook. "Nothing from Brian, I'll check Steve." She suddenly sat up straight, "He's coming down, Debs."

"When?"

"On Thursday. There's a very nice post here thanking everyone for their kind messages. He then says he'll be away on Thursday because he's off to Cornwall to pick up Shell and Beat's belongings. Be back late on Friday evening. Oh, and Michelle won't be joining him because Jack is due home on Friday and she's agreed to pick him up at the airport."

"Michelle?"

"His wife or partner, I assume."

"Yes, of course, and we know Jack is the son. Although I wonder where he's been."

"On holiday, I suppose," Hetty returned the phone to her bag, "Looks like we're in for a busy week, Debs."

"We're definitely doing the police station watch then?"

"Yes, and we'll work out the finer details after tracking Zena Marshall tomorrow. Meanwhile, we must also find out more about Pickle's situation and try to establish whether the brake cables were cut or simply snapped."

As they rose to leave, Tess, collecting glasses from the next table lowered her head. "I heard what you just about Pickle and I can tell you that I've just heard that the brake cables were definitely cut and it's assumed with wire cutters."

Lottie was already home when Hetty returned from the Crown and Anchor and on hearing the plans for the following day shared Debbie and her sister's enthusiasm, although she was shocked to hear that Pickle's brakes had been cut deliberately and was less enthusiastic about the police station surveillance on Thursday. In a buoyant mood, she'd had a lovely evening and confessed that Layton's companionship brought a sparkle to her life and she hoped that he'd never ever leave Pentrillick.

Chapter Nineteen

When the occupants of Primrose Cottage sat down to breakfast on Tuesday morning, Jed was chuckling; he'd just heard on the local radio that a hosepipe ban began at midnight. "It's bonkers," he said, "it's raining and we had rain yesterday and the day before."

"Yes, but not enough to do much good," said Lottie, pragmatically. "It's only drizzle and the gardens are still dry if you dig down. Anyway, the ban will be because the reservoirs are low and the last thing we want is to run out of water."

"And there's nothing like a hosepipe ban to guarantee the days of good weather are well and truly over." Hetty was less tolerant than her sister.

Barbara, not wanting a disagreement to take place changed the subject and asked the sisters if they had plans for the day. Lottie did a bit of quick thinking. She couldn't tell the truth because Jed would disapprove, but if she came up with a fabrication that appealed, her daughter and Jed might ask to join them. Knowing Barbara had no interest in gardening, she opted for a horticultural pastime and said she and Hetty were going to Debbie's to help her create a rockery.

"That's a shame because I was going to see if you'd like to join us. Jed and I are going to Trengillion, aren't we, love?"

Jed nodded.

"Trengillion. Where's that?" Hetty was unfamiliar with the name.

"Somewhere on the Lizard peninsula. I was chatting to Sid and Dolly in the pub last night before we had our dinner and they went down there on Sunday and said how nice it is."

"Well, I hope you have a lovely time," said Lottie. "We've never been there or even heard of it but if you come back and say we should then we shall, won't we, Het?"

"Yes, and thank you for thinking of asking us but we really can't let Debs down." Hetty then turned around the conversation by asking Jed and Barbara about their visit to Pentrillick House, the Liddicott-Treens and the wedding.

Barbara and Jed left straight after breakfast and at ten-thirty, Kitty having said, when asked, that she'd love to join in the day's pursuit, called at Primrose Cottage. As they were leaving the house to meet Debbie, they saw Bernie the boatman's wife entering Blackberry Way.

"Hello, Veronica. Out for a walk?" Hetty was curious.

"Yes, and no," She stopped to get back her breath, "I'm hoping your neighbour is in as I've some information that might be useful, you see."

Hetty's eyes widened. "Information?"

"Yes, it's about Pickle coming off his bike. As you know, Bernie and me manned the white elephant stall at the fete and amongst the stuff we had were a few tools someone had donated: including, would you believe, wire cutters. We remember them well, you see, because Bernie said if they didn't sell he'd buy them. Anyway, at the end of the day when we boxed up the few bits that were left I asked him how much the cutters sold for and he said he hadn't sold them. Well, neither had I so we assume someone nicked them."

"And whoever it was might then have used them to snip Pickle's brake cables." Lottie was shocked.

"Precisely. We didn't know the wires had actually been cut 'til this morning when we saw Sid. He heard in the pub

134

last night, you see. Anyway, that's why I'm up here, to see David Bray. I hope he's in."

Hetty looked into their neighbours' driveway. "Well, his car is here so I should imagine he is too."

"Ideal. Better get a move on then in case he's off to work soon."

"Well," said Kitty, as Veronica entered the gates of Hillside, "that's food for thought."

"It is and it makes today's mission even more important," said Hetty.

"How?" Lottie asked as they headed towards the top of Long Lane.

"Because Zena Marshall was at the fete: Debbie and I both saw her. So I reckon Pickle might have seen her up to no good on one of the occasions and she decided to shut him up."

Chewing over known facts the three women arrived in the village where Debbie sat on the wall outside the Crown and Anchor waiting for them. Around her neck hung a pair of binoculars. Hetty gave her the thumbs up. "Good thinking, Debs." She then told of information received from Veronica.

Inside, having just opened up, Jackie stood behind the bar. She was clearly surprised to see the four ladies. Feeling they ought to explain their presence, Hetty gabbled, "We've just popped in for a coffee while we decide what to do for the day, haven't we, girls?"

The other three nodded while keeping an eye on the door leading to the upstairs guest rooms.

"Oh, I thought you were probably going bird-watching," Jackie pointed to the binoculars Debbie had placed on the table.

"What a good idea," gushed Hetty, unconvincingly, as Jackie poured four coffees.

At eleven-fifteen their patience was rewarded when Zena stepped into the bar dressed in shorts and a polka dot shirt. Beneath her arm she held a sketchpad; over her shoulder was a canvas bag. She greeted Jackie, commented on the weather and then left the bar.

"Quick, drink up," hissed Hetty. The three ladies did as asked, noisily pushed back their chairs and after briefly bidding a confused looking Jackie farewell, all scuttled out of the bar in pursuit of their victim.

To their relief, Zena didn't go to her car but instead walked across the campsite and through a gap in the hedge that led onto the cliff path. Keeping their distance, they followed ducking down whenever they thought Zena might glance back. As they passed by the back gardens of Saltwater House, they hunched themselves down in case Layton should be in the garden and call out to them. To their relief there was no sign of him in the nearby flower beds but he was just visible in the vegetable plot where he appeared to be hoeing between rows of onions. Shortly after, the path ran downhill towards a valley and a small cove where a stream ran into the sea. Before she reached a wooden bridge over the stream, Zena stopped near to a signpost saying Cassie's Cove, placed a small towel on a patch of grass, sat down and from her bag took a box of pencils. She then opened up her sketchpad.

Kitty groaned. "We could be here for hours if she's drawing."

"I was just thinking the same," whispered Hetty, "I mean, she's obviously not planning to meet anyone."

Lottie agreed. "Exactly, and if she's just out sketching there's no point in watching her or waiting to see what she does next, so I suggest we go back home."

"I wonder what she's drawing," Debbie lifted the binoculars to her eyes and then gasped. "No way, look, she's drawing the seed head of a hemlock plant. There's one by the bridge." She passed the glasses to Lottie.

"Ah, but is it hemlock or is it cow parsley?" Lottie wasn't convinced either way.

Kitty took a look. "Looks like cow parsley to me."

"Well whatever, it doesn't really matter," said Hetty, "the main thing is she must know a thing or two about wild flowers, botany and stuff like that, so most likely knows how fatal a hemlock leaf can be."

"Yes," agreed Lottie, "but I think after what happened to Beatrice everyone in Pentrillick knows how fatal hemlock can be."

Feeling the need to get out of their suspect's line of vision, should she look back, the four ladies snuggled down on a rough patch of grass behind bracken, gorse and a good sized boulder.

"Let's look at the facts," said Debbie, "We know she's a divorcee and she currently lives in Kent, as did Shelley. Furthermore, she was staying in the pub when both Beatrice and Shelley were murdered."

"And," said Hetty, "she must have come out of the marriage with a few bob because she looks well dressed."

"But if she came out of the marriage with a few bob, surely that would lessen our case for accusing her of seeking revenge against the woman who wrecked her marriage," said Lottie, "Assuming Shelley did, that is."

"Allegedly wrecked her marriage," added Kitty, "until things are proven one has to add allegedly to all suppositions."

Hetty scowled. "But not when we're chatting amongst ourselves, surely. I mean, no-one can hear us."

"Maybe not," Kitty glanced over her shoulders, "but walls have ears and we don't want to be done for libel."

"Point taken," said Debbie, "but let's get back to known facts."

"Well, I suppose she's a similar age to Shelley so that'd be about right for Shelley pinching her man." Even as the words tumbled from Lottie's lips she knew they were silly.

"But more importantly we know she has an interest in wild flowers and she was at the fete on Saturday and could easily have tampered with Pickle's bike," Hetty scrambled to her knees, "I don't know about you three but I think it's time we confronted her. You know, strike while the iron is hot."

"But you can't just go up to her and accuse her." Lottie was appalled at the prospect.

"Why not? She'll most likely be off home this weekend, so time is of the essence." Hetty stood up, "Anyway, I'm not just going to accuse her. I'm going to make a citizen's arrest."

"You what!" Debbie's hand flew to her face. "You can't, Het."

"No you can't. Sit down and don't be silly," hissed Lottie.

"I agree," said Kitty, "besides, you don't know how to make a citizen's arrest."

But Hetty would not listen; her mind was made up. She marched down the path to where Zena sat and then stood over her.

Zena looked up and smiled sweetly. "Hello, lovely day now the rain has passed, isn't it?"

Hetty stood up straight and folded her arms tightly across her chest aware that she had to act fast before she lost her nerve. "Zena Marshall, I'm arresting you for the murder of Shelley Sinclair and possibly Beatrice Cookson too. Oh, and snipping Pickle's brake cables. You do not have to say anything but whatever you umm…umm…well whatever the rest of it is, it applies."

Lottie, Debbie and Kitty wished the ground would open up beneath them.

Zena laughed.

Hetty looked crushed. "It's not funny. I'm deadly serious."

"A citizen's arrest, eh?"

"Yes."

"I see, well let me help you for next time. The wording is - You do not have to say anything but it may harm your defence if you do not mention when questioned something which you later rely on in Court. Anything you do say may be given in evidence. There is more of course depending on the circumstances and nature of the crime."

Hetty opened her mouth to speak but was unable to come up with a relevant response.

Zena meanwhile, calmly laid down her pencil. "May I ask why you think I would murder the two ladies and tamper with the poor man's bicycle? I mean, I never knew either of the ladies until I came down here for a holiday and even then I had no reason to speak with them. Although if I remember correctly we did exchange smiles when the author and I met on the upstairs landing in the pub one morning after the tragic death of her friend. As for the unfortunate cyclist, I've no idea who he is."

"Beatrice was Shelley's cousin not her friend and we know through reading some of Shelley's works that her characters were guilty of extramarital affairs and we believe that Shelley Sinclair was much the same herself as her characters and for that reason we believe that she had an affair with your husband. The result of this was divorce and you, overcome with grief and humiliation, decided to murder Shelley. Beatrice's death was a mistake but you tried again with the disposable barbecue and succeeded. As for Pickle, we reckon you thought he might have seen you put hemlock on the plates and you needed to shut him up."

"Good theory."

"You're admitting it then?"

"No, of course not."

"But you live in Kent, you're divorced, you were at the fete and by staying in the pub you're near to where both ladies died. And, oh yes, you know your wild flowers."

"And the same applies to many other people."

Hetty unfolded her arms and placed her hands on her hips. "So may I ask why you and your husband divorced?"

"You may and I shall answer despite your impertinence. My husband, Gary, and I parted five years ago. It was amicable because he wanted to marry someone else. I understood his dilemma, you see. Gary has since remarried and he and I are still friends. What is more, I very much like his husband."

Hetty's jaw dropped. "His husband!" The colour rose in her face as she grabbed the signpost for support. "Oh, Zena. What can I say? I've never felt so stupid in my life."

"Nor have you ever looked it, Hetty Tonkins." Lottie spoke with vehemence as she, Kitty and Debbie emerged from their hiding place amongst the gorse, bracken and boulder.

"Good gracious me, you're all here."

"We are and we must all apologise to you, Zena, because we all came to the same conclusion although Lottie, Kitty and I would never have confronted you like Hetty did." Debbie sat down on the grass opposite Zena even though it was still damp. Lottie, relieved the accused was smiling, did likewise.

"I accept your apologies but why are you trying to solve the two murder cases? I mean surely that's the job of the police."

Feeling they needed to explain their actions, Hetty told how they had found Shelley dead after she had failed to visit them at Primrose Cottage. She also confessed that they and she in particular, were busy-bodies who enjoyed attempting to solve crimes in the area. To their surprise Zena was fascinated. "Well, if I can come up with anything to help then I'd be delighted to do so."

"Brilliant. Five heads are better than f... Oh no."

"What's up, Debs?" Hetty turned to see where Debbie was looking. "Oh no."

140

"Hello girls. Fancy seeing you here." Paul Fox, stepped onto the footbridge and then turned to Zena: "I hope these ladies aren't bothering you. I know what they're like."

"Do you two know each other?" Hetty was surprised.

"Yes, we were talking in the pub the other night," said Zena. "It seems Paul and I have a lot in common."

Hetty felt her heart sink. Was she jealous?

"I'm intrigued," admitted Debbie. "What do you have in common?"

"Paul's a retired detective inspector and I'm a serving police sergeant."

"You're a police officer!" Hetty sat before her knees gave way.

"Yes, and that's why your citizen's arrest amused me so, but then there's a first time for everything."

"Citizen's arrest!" Paul roared.

Hetty turned to gaze down at the sea, desperate to avoid the look of exasperation in the erstwhile detective inspector's eyes.

Cook Clara Bragg finished her shift at Pentrillick's care home for the elderly at three o'clock but instead of going straight home, she took a plastic bag from her pocket which she hoped to part-fill with blackberries in order to make her favourite pudding, blackberry and apple crumble. On leaving work the previous day she had noticed brambles in the lane opposite the care home laden with unripe fruit but judging by the flattened vegetation on the grass verge she concluded berries may already have ripened and been picked by foragers. Hence, she reasoned that if she were to hop over the gate into the field she would be able to pick berries on the other side of the hedge that previous foragers might have missed.

Once over the gate, she warily looked across the field to make sure no cattle were anywhere nearby. Satisfied that she was safe she then made her way down the hill watching the hedgerow as she went. Before long she reached a bramble laden with lush black fruit and began to pick. As she stepped away, her bag half full, she felt something hard beneath her foot. Assuming it was a stone she glanced down amongst the tufts of yellow grass where to her surprise she saw a pair of wire cutters. As she stretched out her hand to pick them up, it struck her that they might well be the very cutters that had been used to sever the brake cables on Percy Pickering's bicycle. Knowing she must not handle them in case there were fingerprints, she picked a dock leaf, carefully wrapped it around the cutters and placed them in the plastic bag along with her blackberries. While thinking of her next move, she noticed several cows wandering in from an adjoining field. Keen to get away, she ran down the grassy incline until she reached another gate at the bottom of the lane. Once safely out onto tarmac, she ran along the main street to the Crown and Anchor where she hoped someone would have Detective Inspector David Bray's mobile number.

Chapter Twenty

"How was the trip to whatever you said the place was called?" Lottie asked Barbara and Jed as they arrived back at Primrose Cottage just after six.

"Trengillion and it was smashing," said Barbara, taking a seat on the sofa and removing her shoes. "We took a stroll along a lovely beach, had lunch in a lovely old pub and then went for a wander round the churchyard behind it. So much history. Reading some of the gravestones made me feel like I knew them. You know, I imagined what they looked like and felt I was bringing them back to life."

"I know what you mean," said Lottie, "because we like to wander round the churchyard here. I always think it's a pity that so many are cremated these days. I know it's best for the environment because of space and what have you but it seems a shame that in a hundred years' time there will be no gravestones to read other than a few alongside buried ashes as most people opt to scatter the remains of loved ones in favourite places."

Barbara sighed. "Oh dear, I hadn't thought of it like that and yes, it is really sad. Would you like to be buried, Mum or would you rather be cremated?"

"Ugh, not something I want to think about right now."

Seeing the horrified look on her sister's face, caused Hetty to chuckle.

"We were hoping to find some of my ancestors," said Jed, "but didn't have any luck."

"Ancestors?" Hetty's laugh turned to curiosity. "Do you have Cornish blood then?"

"Apparently, yes. According to Mom her family came from somewhere in Cornwall but she doesn't know where. They went out in the eighteen sixties when mining was in decline here. She wasn't able to tell me much and said she wished she'd listened more when her mom used to go on about it."

"So what was the family name?" Lottie asked.

"Vickery, and Mom's great, great, great grandpa or whatever who first went out there was called Denzil."

"Vickery," mused Hetty, "that name rings a bell but I can't think why."

"Perhaps you read it on a gravestone here," suggested Barbara.

Jed's face lit up. "Hey, you could be right. We'll take a look tomorrow."

"Yeah, we will." Barbara turned to Lottie sitting at the table. "So how did the gardening go, Mum?"

"What? Oh, oh yes, the umm rockery. Well, to be honest we didn't do it in the end. It was such a nice day we all went for a walk along the cliff path instead." Lottie knew she had to tell the truth in case someone in the pub let it slip about Hetty's embarrassing citizen's arrest.

On Wednesday morning, Hetty and Lottie went as usual to work in the charity shop. They had purposely avoided the Crown and Anchor the previous evening because they knew Zena Marshall was likely to be there and worse still Paul. For although Zena confessed the whole episode had amused her greatly it wasn't the case with Paul. He was extremely cross and his harsh words had hurt Hetty more than she cared to admit.

Just before lunch, two of the wigwam girls came into the shop. After looking around, Suzy asked, "Do you have any swimsuits?"

"Yes, we do," Lottie led the girls to a box beneath a shoe rack, "Did you forget to bring one with you?"

"No, I've a beauty but I hung it on the hedge behind our tent to dry and didn't see the thorns. When I pulled it off it tore a damn great hole in it. I wouldn't bother this late in our holiday because we're going back to Reading on Saturday but since the weather's looking good tomorrow I thought it'd be nice to spend a bit of time on the beach."

Lottie tutted, "Must have been either blackthorn or hawthorn. Both have pernicious spikes. Anyway, here we are."

While Suzy looked through the box, Gretel turned to Hetty. "Was it you who attempted to arrest Zena Marshall yesterday?"

Hetty groaned. "Yes it was, but how do you know?"

"Everyone was talking about it in the pub last night. Zena said it made her day. We didn't know who they meant at first but when I asked Tess on the bar she told us it was one of the ladies who had found Shelley and you fitted the description."

"Fitted the description! I hope it was flattering."

Gretel laughed. "Well, yes and no. Tess said you wore brightly coloured floral leggings and pretty tunic tops."

Hetty's eyes narrowed. "And the no part?"

"She said you had the loudest voice."

Lottie smothered a smile.

"This one's the right size and I love the colour," Suzy placed a purple swimsuit on the counter and pulled a wallet from the pocket of her shorts.

Eager to hear Hetty's side of the citizen's arrest incident, Gretel continued, "So why did you think Zena murdered the ladies?"

Realising the girls might be able to input some useful knowledge, Hetty explained how they thought the murderer might bear a grudge over a broken marriage. Therefore they were looking for someone whose husband had left her following an affair with Shelley. They knew Zena and her husband had parted. Put two and two together but sadly made five.

"Oh dear," said Gretel.

Suzy frowned. "But surely if that were case the person you need to find is not a wronged wife but a guilty husband who blamed Shelley for his marriage failure and who probably ended up with next to nothing and no-one to cook his dinner and do his washing."

Hetty slapped her forehead. "Duh! How can we have been so daft? Of course you're right. We should be looking for a man not a woman," she turned to Lottie, "I'll ring Debbie and Kitty during our lunch break. This calls for an urgent meeting."

As the girls left the shop, clearly amused, Lottie groaned.

At half past six that evening, Debbie and Kitty arrived at Primrose Cottage to discuss Suzy's observation. However, they were unable to bring up the topic straight away because Jed and Barbara were still in the house and while Barbara changed her outfit ready to go out for a meal, Jed sat in the living room with the ladies where they waffled on about flowers, the weather and whatever came into their heads. When Kitty mentioned it was her turn to do the flowers in church on Sunday, Jed raised his hand. "That reminds me, before we went to Helford today we did as suggested and took a wander round your churchyard here looking for tombstones bearing the name Vickery and we found several."

"I knew I'd seen the name somewhere," said Hetty.

"Vickery," said Kitty, "Why were you looking for Vickerys?"

146

"Because it's the name of my ancestors on my mom's side. Apparently they went over to the States from Cornwall back in the eighteen sixties."

"But that's fascinating. My maiden name was Vickery, you see."

"Of course," said Hetty, "that's why it rang a bell."

"So might you be related?" Debbie was intrigued.

"Possibly," said Kitty, "distant relatives anyway. Do you have any names and dates, Jed?"

"Only Denzil. He was my mom's grandpa with several greats before his name and it was him that went out to the States."

"Hmm, interesting. I know a bit of my family history but don't recall seeing any Denzils."

"Jackie might be able to help you," said Lottie, "after all, it was her research that helped Norman find his roots."

"Good idea. I'll ask her next time I'm in the pub."

Shortly after, Barbara entered the room wearing a new dress bought on the recent trip to Truro. "Ready, love?"

Jed jumped up. "Yep, and while we're driving I'll tell you the latest Vickery news."

"Right," said Hetty, as they heard the hired car drive away, "Let's get down to business."

The ladies rose from their seats and took up places around the table where Hetty had already placed a notebook and pen. She opened it up and at the top of the page wrote *Men.*

"So where do we start?" Debbie asked.

"With men who have appeared on the scene this year, I suppose," said Kitty, "And especially ones this summer."

Lottie scowled. "Not many to choose from then. I know there have been plenty down on holiday but I can only think of two and they're Claude Dexter and Happy Harper."

"Well, it's a start," Hetty wrote the two names down. "And it might be worth looking into Claude's past. I mean, we know it's Simone's second marriage and that her husband died, but he might well have been married before too."

"I agree," said Debbie, "but I think we can rule out Happy Harper because he says he's never been married."

"He might not be telling the truth," reasoned Hetty.

"No, it couldn't be him, he strikes me as the gentle, artistic sort," said Debbie, "although I suppose it's possible he's a dark horse."

"Well whatever, we'll keep him on the list for now."

"Just remembered another chap here this summer," said Debbie, "The bloke at Sea View Cottage, Joseph something or other."

"Joseph Baker. No, he's too old. Also, he wasn't around when Beatrice died and had only been here for a couple of days when Shelley died. What's more, his wife, Mary, was a godsend at the fete," Lottie reminded her, "I don't know how we'd have managed had she not come to our aid."

"She was a bit bossy though," said Hetty. "She kept telling me what to do."

"Maybe," said Lottie, "but she was very efficient."

"How about Harry's friends, Jack and Jake?" Kitty suggested.

"Too young," said Hetty. "We're looking for people over thirty or more likely over forty."

Kitty tutted. "Of course. Shame though because it limits it somewhat."

Debbie giggled. "You're right there, Kitty because the only other one I can think of is Layton Wolf."

Lottie gave Debbie a withering look. "I won't even respond to that."

"I think we need to widen our time scale," mused Kitty, "you know, consider people who have moved here in recent years because it could well be someone who had their marriage wrecked years ago and seeing Shelley here brought back all the bitter memories."

Hetty nodded. "Excellent point. Let's make a list of everyone who has moved to Pentrillick in the last six years."

"Why six years?" Kitty asked.

"Because it'll be six years in December since Lottie and I moved here so we can't go back any further than that."

"Yes, makes sense. I can go way back of course but we'll stick to six."

"Well rather than discuss the whys and wherefores straight away, let's list all new arrivals first and then go through them one by one and delete the unlikely," Debbie suggested.

"I agree, we'll do that," Hetty looked around the table, pen poised waiting for names.

"Sid," said Lottie, "he arrived the first Christmas we were here."

"Okay," Hetty winced as she wrote down his name.

"And our next door neighbour, David Bray," chuckled Lottie.

Hetty wrote down Detective Inspector David Bray.

"Garfield Haddock from the fish and chip shop," said Debbie.

"And pub Landlord, James Dale," Kitty added.

"Robert Oliver," said Lottie.

"Ah, and Norman Williams," said Hetty.

"School teacher Luke thingy. You know, Natalie's husband."

"Burleigh. Luke Burleigh." Hetty wrote down his name.

Kitty tapped her fingers on a table mat: "the only other one I can think of is Jude Sharp but there must be others."

Hetty wrote down Jude's name and then laid down her pen. "Oh dear, I think this must be the daftest list we've ever written."

Debbie nodded. "I agree. Most of them are our friends. What's more they'd be mortified if they knew we even suggested them."

"Then let's go through them and eliminate the obviously innocent," said Kitty, "and start with Jude. Being his landlady I can say hand on heart that he's never been married and he wouldn't hurt a fly."

"Likewise James Dale," said Debbie, "We know he and Ella have been married for twenty-five years because they celebrated their silver wedding anniversary in March and at the time I recall Ella saying they had been childhood sweethearts."

Hetty crossed off Jude and James. "I'm also taking off Norman. He's in his mid-sixties and so a good twenty years older than Shelley was. What's more he's never been married. He told us that from day one."

"So who does that leave us with, Het?" Lottie asked.

"Robert Oliver, Luke Burleigh, Garfield Haddock and David Bray."

"Well you can rule out Robert," said Debbie. "He's in his sixties too and has been married to Sally for donkey's years. What's more, Gideon works with him, they get on very well and I consider my husband to be a good judge of character."

"And you can certainly take out David next door," said Lottie. "He's never been married. Margot, his partner has, but not David."

"And cross out Luke Burleigh too," said Lottie. "His wife Natalie works with Sandra at the care home and Sandra mentioned a while back that she and Bill got married on the same day as Natalie and Luke, so it stands to reason he couldn't have been married before because he's only a young man now."

Hetty agreed and crossed off Luke's name. "Okay, so that just leaves Garfield Haddock, and we know Garfield never married until he met Matilda who was a divorcee."

Debbie groaned. "So after going all round the houses we're back to just two. Claude Dexter and Happy Harper."

"I suppose," reasoned Kitty, "there's always the possibility that we were right first time and it's a woman we need to find rather than a man."

"True," mused Hetty, "although a man would be more inclined to know about cutting brake cables and would be more familiar with wire cutters."

Lottie scowled. "I don't know about that, Het. We have wire cutters amongst our tools in the garage and I daresay most women would know what they're for."

"Yes, I suppose so."

"And we don't know for sure if there's a link between the tampering of Pickle's bike and the deaths of the cousins anyway," said Debbie, "although I'd be surprised if there isn't."

"Looks like everything hinges on us spotting Shelley's brother Steve at a police station tomorrow then, and somehow getting to talk to him." Hetty picked up her pen: "so while we're all together, ladies, how about we write a list of questions to ask him, subtly of course."

Her suggestion was met by a chorus of groans.

The police having received the wire cutters from Clara Bragg, were hopeful they were the tool used to sever the brake cables on Percy Pickering's bicycle but to eliminate fingerprints they needed to ascertain who had donated them to the fete. Two police officers called at the vicarage to interview Vicar Sam who informed them that the donor was unknown because notices posted around the village and through letterboxes asking for offerings stated the church would be unlocked between 10am and 4pm each day for donations to be left at the back of the church by the door leading into the belfry. Thus they had no idea who had left what. However, once word got round that the police were looking for the donor, Betsy Triggs, the elderly widow who lived next door to Sea View Cottage, said the tools had

151

belonged to her late husband, Eric. She had kept them since his death for sentimental reasons but on hearing of the request for donations decided it was time to let them go and for someone else to make use of them. Consequently, Betsy's fingerprints were taken as were those of stallholders Bernie and his wife, Veronica. Once the three were eliminated, just one clear print amongst a few smudges remained and the police drew a blank. For though it was likely the prints would be a match with the thief-cum-saboteur, without a suspect there was no-one to take prints from and it would be an impossible task to take prints from everyone who attended the fete. Then there was the question of why someone had tampered with Mr Pickering's bicycle. Was it a neighbour who bore a grudge? A malicious act by someone who didn't even know to whom the bicycle belonged? Or was it done by someone who thought Mr Pickering might have witnessed a criminal act towards either Ms Sinclair or her cousin Mrs Cookson? One thing was for sure. The brake wires would have been cut after Mr Pickering arrived at the fete simply because he had ridden there safely.

Chapter Twenty-One

On Thursday morning, Hetty sat at the dining table in the sitting room gazing from the window.

"What are you looking at?" Lottie placed a mug of coffee in front of her sister.

"Shush. A little trotty wagtail."

"Ah! '*Little trotty wagtail, he waddled in the mud, and left his little footmarks, trample where he would. He waddled in the water-pudge, and waggle went his tail*', I can't remember the next bit."

"*And chirruped up his wings to dry upon the garden rail*," continued Hetty, "Although that wasn't the first verse, was it?"

"No, the second but my favourite," Lottie sat down at the table, "Brings back happy memories of Mum getting us to learn it. She was very proud of John Clare, the Northamptonshire poet, wasn't she?"

"Yes, she was. Funny isn't it that as we get older, childhood memories are very special. And we did have a happy childhood, didn't we, Lottie?"

"We did. In fact I've had a happy life and I think you have too."

"I have but when you say it like that it sounds as though we've on our last legs. We're only seventy and there's still a lot of life left in us both. At least I hope there is."

"Are you alright, Het? It's just you sound a bit, well, maudlin."

"Yes, I'm fine. It's just I feel that things are about to change. You know, we've come to the end of an era."

"Change? Not for the worse, I hope."

"No, not at all, and probably for the best. It's just, well, you know it's the old thing. Some of us don't like change, especially when we get older and set in our ways."

Norman, with just one more day's work at Saltwater House stopped for a break mid-morning to ease his aching back. As instructed by Layton, he went to the kitchen to make himself coffee which as the weather was fine and sunny he intended to drink outside. On the work surface, Layton had also left a selection of chocolate bars from which Norman was welcome to help himself. As he made the coffee he saw from the kitchen window that Layton's car was not parked on the gravel. He turned to Clarence. "Layton's not back yet then?"

"Layton loves Lottie," said Clarence.

Norman was rather surprised. "Does he now?"

"Where's Lottie?" Clarence asked.

Before Norman could answer, Pickle entered the kitchen also to make coffee. He had called in to see Layton and check how the garden had fared in his absence.

"Hello, Pickle. Good to see you."

"Thanks. It's good to be out."

"Where's Lottie?" Clarence chattered.

Norman chuckled. "That bird's a character. He reckons Layton loves Lottie. Any truth in it, do you think?"

"It wouldn't surprise me. Lottie often pops in; occasionally with Hetty but usually on her own. Not that I've been here to see her for a day or two of course."

"Here, let me make you coffee." Seeing Pickle was struggling, Norman reached for a clean mug.

"Thanks."

"So, how are you? You look well enough."

"I'm alright. Just a couple of broken ribs and a dodgy wrist. Had a bit of concussion but the doctors have given me the all clear, thank goodness, and just told me to rest. The neighbours have been fussing over me, feeding me and what have you but there's only so much resting a chap can do and I was going stir crazy looking at four walls. That's why I came down here. Partly to see how the garden's doing and partly to stretch my legs."

"Have you seen Layton then?"

"Yes, he was just popping out when I arrived. Said he wouldn't be long but couldn't stop because he had an appointment with the optician. I said I'd hang around 'til he got back and he said to make myself at home. He mentioned you were here too. So how's the job going?"

"Nearly done. So what do you think happened to your bike?"

"Obviously sabotage, but who did it and why I've no idea. The coppers reckon I might have witnessed something to do with the two cousins who died but if I did I've no idea what."

"How about your bike? Is it fixable?"

Pickle shook his head. "Sadly not. My neighbours tried to straighten the front wheel and frame but eventually gave up. It looks a mess so I'll take what's salvageable off for spares and scrap the rest." He chuckled, "Amazingly, the fuchsias I bought at the fete survived the impact although a few bits got broken off. As for my bike, I need to get back to work soon to earn some dosh so I can save up for another, but for now I'll have to make do with my legs."

"Well, at least the weather's not too bad for walking at the moment and it's a damn sight cooler than it has been." As Norman handed Pickle his coffee, an idea popped into his head.

The ladies calculated that it would take roughly six to six and a half hours for Shelley's brother Steve to drive from his home in Kent to West Cornwall. And working on the assumption he would leave no earlier than six in the morning they estimated his time of arrival would be any time after midday. For that reason they planned to group at Primrose Cottage at eleven and then drive in two separate cars to their designated police stations to begin their surveillance.

They left Blackberry Way at eleven-thirty having agreed that Kitty would go with Hetty to Helston to watch the police station there, and Lottie would go with Debbie to do the same in Camborne. The purpose of their visit was to watch the car parks and front entrances and if Steve was spotted to notify the other team, see when he left and then follow him. Because they knew through his Facebook message that he would not be home until late on Friday they assumed his next move would be to go wherever he planned to stay overnight. Once done they would sit in their cars and wait for him to leave said premises when hopefully he would go out for a drink or something to eat. If this was the case they would pursue him further. The object of their mission was to bump into him accidently on purpose and get him talking about his sister and any persons who might hold a grudge against her or with whom she had been in conflict.

Deep down Lottie thought the operation was a complete waste of time because Steve would already have been questioned by the police, and Beatrice's husband, Brian, likewise. A sentiment shared by Kitty. But not wanting to dampen the enthusiasm of Hetty and Debbie, they went along with the plans for a quiet life.

To avoid drawing suspicion to their repetitious lurking, they took with them numerous items to alter their appearances. This included, differing styles of jackets and cardigans; hats and headscarves in all shapes and sizes, and sunglasses in various designs and colours. All were thankful that the sun was shining thus meaning they would not look out of place wearing said sunglasses and sunhats.

Once they reached the premises they were to observe, the drivers of each car parked as near as possible in residential areas away from any CCTV cameras that might be in the vicinity of the police stations. To begin the process, Debbie was first to take her position in Camborne and Hetty in Helston.

On the upper floor of the police station in Helston, Detective Inspector David Bray, having arrived from Camborne for a meeting with colleagues, was given a cup of coffee, and as the sun was shining he walked towards the window to benefit from the sun's heat. To put sugar in his coffee he placed his mug on the window ledge and glanced down to the road below where to his surprise he spotted his next door neighbour, Hetty Tonkins, standing alone and frequently looking at her watch. Assuming she was waiting to meet someone he thought nothing more, drank his coffee and then met up with his colleagues. However, after the meeting, wondering if she had met whoever, he looked again from the window only this time to see another of his neighbours, Kitty Thomas, acting in the same manner but a little further along the road from where Hetty had stood. Puzzled he had another coffee and then collected together various papers. Before he left the premises, through curiosity he looked out again. "Oh this is daft," he said to himself.

"What's daft, sir?" asked a young police sergeant.

"Sorry, I was thinking out loud." He frowned: "well no actually, tell me what you think." He then explained the movements of his neighbours.

"Perhaps you're mistaken, sir, and one or both of them might not be your neighbours."

David Bray shook his head. "No, I don't think so. Hetty Tonkins might think she's changing her appearance by swapping sun hats and wearing different coloured cardigans and what have you but it doesn't fool me."

However, when he left the building neither of his neighbours was to be seen. The reason being, they were in the throes of changing watch inside Hetty's car.

Meanwhile, in Camborne, Debbie and Lottie were acting in the same manner as their counterparts in Helston, and it was while Debbie was watching the police station that she spotted Happy Harper enter the building. Seeing it as a development of sorts, she sent a text to Hetty telling of her observation. Hetty, sitting in her car parked in Station Road, drinking coffee from a flask while Kitty took her turn watching for Steve Sinclair, sent a message back suggesting Debbie make a note of how long he was in there and they would discuss it later at the Crown and Anchor.

By four o'clock patience was wearing thin. Happy Harper was in Camborne police station for twenty-two minutes and that was the only bit of excitement Debbie and Lottie experienced. Similarly in Helston the watch had been fruitless.

At ten minutes past four, Debbie returned to her car and faced Lottie in the passenger seat. "I don't know about you, Lottie, but I've had enough and I think we ought to call it a day."

"Hallelujah! I'd had enough three hours ago."

"Good, I'll ring Hetty and see what she thinks."

Hetty and Kitty agreed the whole episode had been very tedious and as they had missed lunch suggested they make their way back to Primrose Cottage for a cup of tea and a sandwich to plan their next move. They would then meet up later at the Crown and Anchor to see if there had been any developments in the village during their absence.

After their refreshments, Debbie drove home to St Mary's Avenue in order to tell her husband, Gideon she was back but not stopping, as, after changing her clothes she was going to the pub to meet up with Hetty, Lottie and Kitty. Gideon was himself preparing to go out for a parochial church council meeting at the vicarage.

Hetty, worried about going to the pub after her embarrassing citizen's arrest, but knowing she had to face everyone sooner or later, walked down Long Lane with

Kitty and her sister in silence. Kitty sensing her discomfort told her not to worry as most people would have already forgotten and those who remembered would be tactful enough to keep their thoughts to themselves. When they reached the bottom of the hill they saw Debbie was already there and sitting in her usual place on the low wall. She stood as they approached her and all walked in together.

Inside the pub, Kitty took her purse from her handbag. "I'll get the drinks while you go and find a table."

After expressing their thanks they glanced around the room looking for somewhere to sit. When Hetty glimpsed the back of Paul's head, she panicked. "Looks a bit busy in here. Let's go out on the sun terrace." Without waiting for the others to respond she quickly led them through the French doors to a vacant table in the corner overlooking the beach.

"Kitty won't see us out here so I'll go and tell her where we are." Lottie placed her handbag on the back of a chair and returned to the bar.

"Are you alright, Het?" Debbie asked, "It's just you look a bit pale."

"Yes, yes, I'm fine."

A chair scraped on the wooden decking. "I thought it was you. I recognised your voice, Hetty." At the next table sat Mary and Joseph.

"Oh, hello, Mary, didn't see you there. Thanks again for your help at the fete."

"You're very welcome. I like to make myself useful."

"Pleased to hear it and are you enjoying your holiday?"

"Yes, very much thank you," Mary leaned back her chair: "Was it you who tried to arrest the police lady? Joseph reckons it wasn't, but I'm sure it was because I heard someone say the name Hetty so that has to be you."

Hetty felt her face burning. "Yes, it was but I can assure you I have apologised profusely and been forgiven."

"No need to apologise, love. We all make mistakes and most folk think you're a star for being concerned. And that includes me. I'm a great believer in justice and think we all ought to do more to make the world a better and safer place."

"Oh, well, yes, thank you. But I'm not sure that accusing someone of a murder they clearly didn't commit comes into the category of making the world a better and safer place."

As a waitress arrived with food for Mary and Joseph, Kitty and Lottie returned with a tray of drinks.

"I see Paul's in there, and Layton too. At least I think it's them. Can't be too sure though as it's very busy and they're in the dimly lit bit." Kitty sat down just as Paul appeared in the doorway.

"Are you lot avoiding us? I saw you come in but you scuttled out here before I could beckon you over."

"No, we're not avoiding you, are we, girls?" Hetty hoped she sounded convincing.

"Good, because Layton and I are chatting with someone I'm sure you'd like to meet. And he'd like to meet you."

"Really! Who's that?" Kitty couldn't recall seeing anyone of interest at their table.

"Steve Sinclair. Shelley's brother."

Hetty's jaw dropped. "You mean he's in there and with you?"

"Yes, and he's keen to meet anyone who met his sister."

"No way. So we spent all afternoon lurking outside police stations looking like lemons and he was here all the time. What a fool I am." Hetty didn't know whether to laugh or cry.

"Don't be daft, it's not your fault," sympathised Debbie, "You were on the right track but just got the location wrong."

Paul frowned. "You've been lurking outside police stations! Why?"

Hetty whimpered.

"So why is Steve here?" Lottie hurriedly asked. She obviously knew the reason but wanted to avoid having to answer Paul's question.

"To pick up Shelley and Beatrice's belongings. The police dropped them off here earlier today after Steve told them he'd booked a room and intended to stay for the night rather than drive back the same day. But you've not answered my question. Why were you outside police stations?"

Hetty sighed. "We were hoping to see Steve go in to pick the tent and stuff up. Then when he came out we'd follow him and if the chance arose ask a few questions. It was my idea, so don't blame the others."

"No surprise there then. But how would you have recognised him?"

"Because I saw his picture on Facebook when looking for Beatrice's husband, Brian. And before you comment I wasn't being nosy, Paul. I, we, just wanted to send our condolences. This was a few days ago."

"And did you? Send condolences, that is."

"Yes, and in his reply Brian mentioned Shelley's brother, Steve and that's how we got to know about him."

"How come you and Layton are chatting to him?" Debbie asked, "I mean surely you didn't look him up on Facebook."

"No, I didn't need to. David Bray asked me to pick him up in Penzance so I could bring him back here. He came down by train, you see, to enable him to drive his sister's car home. The car's outside now. I'm surprised you didn't see it. I mean, you don't see many Morris Travellers these days."

"He came down by train!" gasped Hetty, "What numpties we are. We'd forgotten about Shelley's car, hadn't we, girls?"

The 'girls' rolled their eyes.

"Anyway, when you're ready come and join us."

"We will," said Lottie.

"Does that mean you're not cross with Het?" Debbie quickly asked as he turned to leave.

Paul laughed. "Cross! No, I'm not cross. Not anymore, anyway. But I really think Miss Tonkins needs taking in hand."

Hetty was taken aback when Lottie, Kitty and Debbie nodded in agreement.

"Phew, we got off lightly there," sighed Kitty, as Paul left the sun terrace. "I thought we were in for a right telling off."

"Yes, just as well he doesn't know about our two latest suspects," said Debbie. "They're both in by the way and I've been watching them through the open French doors. Neither have done anything suspicious though. Having said that, they're hardly likely to, are they?"

"Our two suspects?" Lottie was momentarily confused.

"Claude Dexter and Happy Harper."

"Oh, yes, of course. Due to today's tiresome drag, I'd forgotten all about them."

"Yes, it was rather a drag," conceded Debbie, "but at least we saw Happy, and now we need to find out why he was at Camborne nick. I mean, was his visit voluntary or had he been ordered to go in?"

"Goodness only knows," Hetty glanced over to where Claude Dexter sat with his MP wife, "And what do we do about Claude? We need to get chatting to him but I don't like Simone so we can't barge in and make small talk."

"I don't think she likes us either," chuckled Debbie, "not after what she said the other night."

Kitty frowned. "I'm trying to remember if I ever saw Claude speaking to Shelley. You know, if there seemed any animosity between them or something like that."

"Hmm, I can't say as I ever saw them together," mused Lottie. "On the other hand, Happy often chatted with Shelley and Beatrice, so I really think we can rule him out.

I mean, they obviously got on well and if there had been a relationship in the past that had resulted in Happy losing a wife, then that wouldn't have been the case, would it?"

"Very true, and I think it's daft to even consider him," agreed Debbie, "despite his whereabouts this afternoon. He seems a really nice bloke and I think his shock and sadness when both ladies died was one hundred percent genuine."

"He was at the fete though," Hetty reminded them, "and so was Claude because Simone opened it."

Lottie scowled. "What's the fete got to do with anything?"

"Pickle's bike," Hetty reminded her, "you're not really with it tonight, are you?"

Debbie chuckled. "I bet that's because she's itching to go and sit with Layton."

Lottie opened her mouth to object and then smiled. "Yes, you're quite right. The sun is fast disappearing from here now, so drink up ladies. I think it's time to move and introduce ourselves to Steve."

The conversation that followed with Paul, Layton and Steve, although enjoyable, did not in any way help the ladies, clue wise, in their quest to find who was responsible for the deaths of Shelley and Beatrice. Steve said that Shelley's emails had been checked by the police and none were threatening. Likewise her social media posts had been scrutinised and friends, relatives and neighbours questioned but no source revealed even a trace of animosity.

Chapter Twenty-Two

On Friday morning, disaster struck. Hetty was in the kitchen washing the breakfast dishes and happily singing, relieved to be back in Paul's good-books. Lottie, meanwhile, was in the sitting room dusting and watering her aspidistra before they went to work in the charity shop. As she returned the plant to its place on the sideboard, the phone in the hallway rang. Having dry hands, Lottie answered. The caller, clearly distressed, gabbled a greeting.

"Oh, hello, Debs. What's up?"

"Fire. Gideon just rang to say there's a fire at Pentrillick House. It's in the east wing and was well alight when he arrived for work at half eight this morning. There are four fire engines on the scene." Debbie paused for breath.

"But that's terrible, Debs. Is there anyone trapped inside?"

"I don't think so. Not now at least. Tristan and Samantha were inside when it started and have been taken away by ambulance. Gideon said they tried to save some of the family paintings and treasures but got trapped inside the ballroom when something well alight fell across the doorway."

"Oh my goodness. Are they hurt or is it just smoke inhalation?"

"Both, I think. The burns aren't life threatening but from what's being said they look nasty and are mostly to the hands and feet. They had bare feet you see. The smoke alarm raised them and so they threw on their dressing gowns and went to salvage what they could before the fire brigade arrived."

Lottie sat down on the bottom step of the staircase. "How about Jemima and Jeremy. Were they there?"

"No, thank goodness. They're away on holiday with friends."

"That's something I suppose."

"It is, but what about the wedding?"

"Oh, good heavens that never even crossed my mind. I must ring Bill and tell him. Speak later Debs and thanks for letting us know."

Lottie's hands shook as she phoned her son Bill, having briefly explained the situation to Hetty. Bill then rang Zac. Zac, who was just leaving home for work, passed on the news to his fiancée, Emma. Emma wasn't due at Pentrillick House until ten-thirty but on hearing the news wanted to go straight away to see if she could help at all. Zac, not wanting her to go alone, rang Sid to tell him the news and say he'd be late for work.

Other than garden staff no other of the estate's employees was in, as the grounds didn't open up to the public until eleven o' clock. With tears streaming down her face and Zac holding her tight, Emma watched through a haze of flashing blue lights as smoke and flames spilled from the windows of the house she adored.

For much of the morning, talk in the charity shop was about the fire, with everyone seeking out the latest news. Shortly before the sisters closed for lunch, Sid entered the shop with his fingers crossed hoping they would have a toaster for sale.

"You're in luck," Lottie pointed to the shelf above the bookcase, "It only came in the other day and has passed its safety check."

"Brilliant," Sid took the toaster from the shelf. "I just got back from work and fancied beans on toast but my perishing thing wouldn't work. I'll get it fixed if I can.

Meanwhile, this will do nicely." Sid took a five pound note from his wallet and laid it on the counter.

"Have you finished for the day then?" Hetty asked. "I'm wondering about Zac, you see."

"Yep, but Zac hasn't worked at all today. He rang this morning, you see, to say he was driving Emma to Pentrillick House and he'd join me later. I told him not to worry as the job we're on would be all done and dusted by lunchtime and I didn't think it worth starting another, especially on a Friday and with it being a Bank Holiday weekend. Zac was obviously relieved as he'd be able to stay with Emma. Needless to say the poor kid's very upset. In fact, from the quiver in Zac's voice this morning, I'd say they both are."

"Of course, of course." Lottie put the note in the till. "It's not just Emma's place of work, is it though? It's the venue for their wedding too and I know the poor girl loves that house and is very fond of Tristan and Samantha."

"Understandable," said Sid, "the house is impressive and it, and the Liddicott-Treens, are a great asset to the village."

"Is there any more news about the fire?" Hetty asked, "Like what was the cause?"

"I've no idea what the cause was but I do know that it's out now and the building itself has stood up pretty well. Most of the damage appears to be to the contents and thankfully it didn't spread through the whole house. In fact, from what I've heard, it didn't spread far at all."

"That's good and at least no lives were lost," said Lottie.

"Yes, that is a blessing." Hetty picked up the crystal ball. "I know it's going off subject and you'll probably think me daft, but while you're here, Sid, will you take a look into this and tell me what you see? I ask because you dabbled with spiritualism a few years back."

"Oh, I've heard about this thing from young Zac. His dad reckons you're all loopy."

166

"Hmm, that's a bit rich coming from someone who asks a tortoise for advice." Hetty was indignant.

"Yeah," chuckled Sid, "I've heard about that too. Tim, or whatever he's called." He looked down at the ball Hetty had placed in front of him, "Well, I better do it justice and go into Psychic Sid mode even though he was a bumbling amateur." Sid closed his eyes and waved his hands over the ball. When he opened them, he chuckled. "I must have lost the knack, cos all I can see is the reflection of my ugly mug."

Lottie laughed. "I never see anything either."

"Oh, why is it that I see things then?" Hetty was clearly disappointed with Sid's verdict.

"I think, Hetty, you must have an active imagination and you'll find that when you look into a crystal ball you see what you want to see."

Lottie chuckled. "That figures. When Het asked it who took the lives of Beatrice and Shelley, she saw Simone Dexter's face."

"What, the MP? I take it you don't like her then."

Hetty scowled and so Lottie answered. "You're right. Het doesn't like her because she told us we drink too much."

"Ouch!" Chuckling to himself, Sid left the shop with the toaster beneath his arm.

Chapter Twenty-Three

Friday night was busy at the Crown and Anchor. For the wigwam girls their holiday was fast nearing its end as they were due to return home to Reading the following morning. Happy Harper, likewise was in for the last time, as were Simone Dexter, the Member of Parliament and her cartoonist husband, Claude. In her room above the bar, Zena Marshall's bags were packed to enable her to leave straight after breakfast the next morning, and for locals, Friday night was always an occasion to celebrate the end of a working week and in this case also to welcome a Bank Holiday weekend.

Throughout the evening much talk was of the fire at Pentrillick House and the effect it would have on Zac and Emma's wedding. They learned, however, that the wedding would go ahead as planned but at a different venue. For James and Ella on hearing the news had promptly offered the use of the Crown and Anchor's field to house the reception. By then the school holidays would be coming to an end and anyone wishing to camp could still be accommodated at the far end of the field. This was possible because the Pentrillick House marquee was not damaged by the fire and the Liddicott-Treens, concerned about their event's manager's special day, were only too happy for it to be used for the occasion.

"So, how are they?" Hetty asked Zac, shortly after they arrived at the Crown and Anchor, as both stood at the bar buying drinks: "the Liddicott-Treens, that is."

"They'll be okay, which is more than can be said for the house. Emma went to see them this afternoon in hospital with another member of staff and she said they seemed more concerned about our wedding than their own well-being. As far as the house is concerned it's unlikely it'll open up to the public again much before Christmas."

"Oh dear. So the Christmas Wonderland might not take place this year."

"Maybe not but it's early days yet and if I know Tristan and Samantha, they'll do everything they can to ensure it goes ahead. We'll know more tomorrow anyway because they're both due to be released from hospital then."

"It sounds like they're coping well."

"Hmm, maybe, but Em said through the stiff upper lip and all that you can see that they're actually gutted. But then the place is insured and as long as the paintings and antiques aren't too badly damaged I see no reason why they can't be restored to their former glory."

"Let's hope so." Hetty paid for her drinks order and slipped her bank card back inside her purse, "Is there any word as to how the fire started?"

"Not yet," Zac looked over his shoulder, "and I shouldn't really say this, but from their bedroom window Samantha saw someone running across the lawns shortly before the alarms went off and she smelled smoke. She watched as they slipped through a gap in the hedge and then heard a car out in the lane drive off, so it's possible it was arson. But keep that under your hat for now because it's not common knowledge yet." Zac picked up his pint of beer and Emma's gin and tonic.

Hetty patted her lips. "Mum's the word."

With drinks in hand, Zac returned to the joined tables where Emma sat with Harry, Jake, Jack and the wigwam girls. Hetty, glad to see the youngsters getting on well together, returned to Lottie, Debbie and Kitty, sitting over by the open French doors.

"We were just saying, Het, that we think the chances of us sussing out what went on with Shelley and Beatrice are fast slipping away," said Debbie, "I mean, if Claude Dexter and Happy Harper are going home tomorrow then there will be no suspects left."

"And as we've already said we don't think it was either of them anyway," admitted Lottie.

As Hetty was about to respond, Paul Fox placed his pint of beer on their table and took a seat between Hetty and Kitty. "Mind if I join you?"

"Looks like you already have," chuckled Debbie.

He grinned. "Well I thought I better come over and make sure you're not up to no good."

"Cheeky," tutted Hetty.

"As a matter of fact," said Debbie, "we were just saying we think this summer's cases will go unsolved. Unsolved by us anyway."

"Music to my ears. You playing a part, that is," Paul took a sip of beer, "So may I ask who your poor suspects are or were? Apart from Zena of course but we'll say no more about that."

"Well," said Hetty, trying to sound efficient, "we've now ruled out it being a female with a broken marriage and decided to look instead for a male with a broken marriage but after much toing and froing we were only able to come up with two names. The first is Happy Harper..."

"...Happy," laughed Paul, "Well I can tell you for a fact that Happy has never been married. Which reminds me I must ask him if he got his wallet back okay."

"Wallet?" Hetty was puzzled.

"Yes, he lost it the other day while out shopping but luckily for him someone found it and handed it in to Camborne Police Station. He was going to collect it yesterday."

All four ladies remained quiet.

"So who is your other suspect?" Paul asked, surprised by their muted voices.

"Oh, Claude. Claude Dexter," said Debbie.

"Claude! Definitely not him. Claude's first and only wife is Simone."

"Hmm, and Simone's marriage didn't fail," said Lottie, "because her husband died."

"Not quite true," admitted Paul, "Simone's first husband died but her second marriage failed and ended in divorce."

Debbie's eyes flashed. "Second marriage! So is Claude her third husband?"

Paul nodded.

"And the reason for the breakup of the second marriage?" Hetty eagerly asked.

Paul winced. "It was infidelity on his part."

Hetty sat up straight. "I knew it. So it's her. It's Simone. The crystal ball was right. You must arrest her, Paul, before she goes home."

"Hang on a minute, it's not that simple. For a start I'm no longer a serving officer and if I were I'd need evidence."

Hetty ignored him. "I'll ask Zena then. She said she'd help if she could."

Paul grabbed her arm. "You'll do no such thing."

"I'll Google the wretched woman then," Hetty took her phone from her handbag, "Being an MP she's bound to be on Wikipedia or something like that. I'll see if it mentions her past and stuff like marriage."

No-one spoke as Hetty found the desired article and read through its contents. Finally she laid her phone down on the table. "She comes from up-north so not the right area and her husband's affair was with a woman, now his wife, who I've never heard of."

Paul nodded. "Exactly. You must learn, Het, to live by the old adage: act in haste and repent at leisure." He squeezed her hand, "But I have to admit, I admire your enthusiasm."

Standing at the bar, Bill with Crumpet, the Old Bakehouse dog by his feet, was ordering drinks for himself,

Sandra, Barbara and Jed, when Norman having just arrived squeezed in a gap by his side.

"Hey, Bill, I had a surprise yesterday when I was told that Layton Wolf's quite besotted with your mum. Any truth in it, do you know?"

"Really! Now that is interesting. She certainly mentions him a lot and I know she often goes down there but assumed Auntie Het went too. So who did you hear it from?"

Norman felt his face flush. "Clarence, the parrot," he chuckled.

As the evening wore on the wigwam girls became more boisterous; because they were due to return home the next day they would not be running before they left, so they drank more than usual. Gretel, the noisiest of the four, reached inside the pocket of her jacket draped across the back of a chair for her mobile phone to take pictures of their last night. After taking several of themselves, Gretel urged everyone to crowd in for a group picture and she asked Jackie behind the bar to take two or three for her. Jackie duly obliged. People then gathered around the table and watched the screen of Gretel's mobile to make sure they looked presentable on Jackie's handiwork. After which Gretel scrolled through earlier pictures much to the amusement and embarrassment of her friends.

"Go back to the ones you took when we first arrived," said Hannah, "I want to be reminded of the nightmare we went through putting up the wigwam."

Diane groaned. "Well at least we know it's easier to take down than it is to put up, thanks to the lads who helped when we had to move it after Mrs Cookson died." She cast a glance of appreciation towards Harry and his two friends.

Hetty's ears had pricked up. A picture of the girls pitching the wigwam might show Shelley and Beatrice's tent too. Curious to see if it did, she peered over Gretel's shoulder. The girls laughed as the pictures lit up the screen but it was the one that followed which caught Hetty's attention.

"Hemlock," she squealed, "Why have you taken a picture of a hemlock plant?"

Gretel laid her phone on the table and turned to face Hetty. "Simple. I saw it growing down by a stream when we were out running one day and wondered if that's what it was. Bearing in mind what had happened to poor Mrs Cookson. I took it so that when I got back I could Google it. Couldn't do it while running as I was already at the back of us four and didn't want to get left behind."

"I see, then once identified you'd know to avoid it," reasoned Hetty. "Very wise of you."

Gretel smiled sweetly. "Precisely. I read that it's really nasty and when you go running here there and everywhere like we do it pays to be alert."

Diane sitting beside Gretel picked up the phone, a look of confusion on her face. "You're lying."

"What! Why do you say that?" A scowl replaced Gretel's smile.

"Because the pictures taken after the hemlock one are of us eating here in the pub. And look, there in the background are Shelley Sinclair and her cousin."

Gretel shrugged her shoulders. "So!"

Hetty gasped. "So Beatrice was alive and well when you took the hemlock picture. How do you explain that, young lady?"

The bar fell silent as all eyes focused on Gretel, who with obvious unease, slowly stood, kicked aside her chair and backed away towards the door. A quick glance over her shoulder, indicated she planned to escape. To stop her, a small gathered of people grouped together to block her path. Panic-stricken, she paused, reached for an empty bottle and smashed it hard against the edge of a table. Everyone gasped as she then leapt forward and with her free hand grabbed Hetty by the scruff of the neck. As Hetty struggled and stumbled backwards, Gretel pushed the jagged bottle edge against her cheek. "Stand back all of you unless you want to go to a funeral next week as well as a wedding."

"Het," whispered Lottie, as she lowered herself down onto the floor before her legs gave way. Barbara attempted to go to her mother's aid but a warning look from Gretel stopped her. Feeling faint, Kitty unable to breath, watched as a trickle of blood ran down Hetty's neck.

No-one dared move or so it seemed. But Debbie with flushed cheeks and thumping heart, felt her adrenaline rising. With piercing eyes she glared at Gretel's menacing face and slowly rose from her seat. On the next table, Sid and Dolly were dining and shocked by the circumstances, Sid's knife and fork were half way twixt his mouth and plate. As he lowered his hands, Debbie snatched the plate from beneath his nose and quickly hurled it through the air. The plate whirled and spun across the bar; scampi and chips flew in all directions and peas rolled across the floor. The plate hit Gretel on the temple and momentarily stunned, she released her grip on Hetty and stumbled backwards. The broken bottle slipped from her hand and grazed her leg as it fell and then smashed on the flagstone floor. Lottie, with renewed vigour, scrambled to her feet and Barbara grabbed Hetty to break her fall. As the girls screamed, Paul leapt forwards, seized Gretel, pulled her arms behind her back and forced her face down onto the nearest table. Jed ran to assist him, and Zena, already on her feet, handed her silk scarf to Jed who with sleight of hand bound Gretel's wrists, held firmly together by Paul. And while James rang the police, Crumpet, the Old Bakehouse dog, gobbled up the unexpected treat of scampi, chips and peas.

Chapter Twenty-Four

Having taken charge of the situation, Paul instructed everyone to remain where they were. Not that anyone had any intention of leaving for all were keen to see what happened next.

Meanwhile, Debbie realising how close her impromptu action could have gone disastrously wrong, eased herself into the nearest chair. Feeling faint, she brushed away tears and rested her head against her trembling cupped hands. Kitty, having recovered from her dizzy spell, sat down beside her and gave her a hug. "Come on, cheer up, Debs. Het's safe now thanks to you. You did well. Really well and we're all ever so proud of you."

Debbie raised her head. "Bless you, Kit, but I can't believe what I did. I mean, it's the crazy sort of thing Hetty would have done." She smiled, "I suppose after all these years her ways are beginning to rub off on me."

Hearing tongues clicking, she turned her head to see the lady in question; her face pale, her eyes moist with tears as she dabbed the graze on her cheek with a napkin; her sister and niece close by her side.

"Thank you, Debs. I'll be forever in your debt. Your quick thinking probably saved my life."

Debbie squeezed Hetty's hand and smiled. "I always knew being top of the class at discus throwing would come in handy one day."

Leaving Paul and Jed to deal with Gretel, Zena asked the ladies if they were alright. They assured her they were.

"This is crazy," said Bill, helping comfort his mother and aunt, "because it looks to me as though those girls are behind the deaths of the poor ladies that died."

Zena nodded. "Well, Gretel anyway. I don't think the other three had anything to do with it."

"All I can say is, thank goodness Shelley's brother only stayed the one night," said Lottie, "I'd have hated him to have witnessed tonight's outburst of emotion."

Around the two tables pushed together where the youngsters had just an hour before been laughing and joking, Gretel's three friends sat in stunned silence, sobered up by the shock of the unexpected circumstances. As for Gretel, realising she was incapacitated by the scarf, she sat mute, her head hung low, having given up the struggle.

Gradually people began to move around and speak, their voices low and little more than whispers. When the police arrived the bar fell silent again. Paul spoke with the officers and then Gretel was taken away. The remaining police then took statements from all who had witnessed the earlier kerfuffle.

It was after midnight when the last police officers left and they were shortly followed by the bulk of the pub's clientele, including Bill and Sandra because Sandra was due to work the early shift at the care home on Saturday morning. Barbara and Jed, however, chose to stay on to escort Hetty and Lottie home when they were ready to leave. The pub had a licence to stay open until one on Fridays and Saturdays and so those who had remained bought more drinks.

"Are you girls alright?" Hetty sat down at their table, a glass of advocaat and brandy bought by Layton in her hand, "You all look very pale."

Diane, her eyes red from crying, answered. "We're in shock but we'll be fine. How about you? We're so sorry for what Gretel did. It was horrible. Are you okay now?"

"Still a little shaken but like you I'll be fine."

"So does this mean that Gretel killed the two ladies?" Suzy asked.

"Sadly, it looks that way, but it's too soon to be sure."

"But why?" Hannah asked, "As far as we're concerned she didn't even know them let alone have a reason to wish them harm."

Debbie, also with advocaat and brandy, sat down beside Hetty. "That's something we'd all like to know."

"Could you help us all?" Zena sat down on the edge of the table, "You know, tell us a bit about her. How you knew her and stuff like that. But before you answer, I must stress I'm asking out of curiosity and not in the capacity of a police officer."

"We'll try," said Hannah.

Suzy looked at her friends. "I'll start, shall I? I mean, I got to know her first."

Diane nodded. "Yes, please do."

Hannah agreed.

Suzy's fingers fiddled with a loose button on her shirt. "Well, I first met Gretel in November I think it was. This was last year of course, and it was at the gym where she's a fitness instructor. After becoming a member I started to go there a couple of times a week. Gretel and me got on well, started meeting up socially and well, became friends. Over the following months, Diane and Hannah, who'd known each other for years, became members too and we all became friends. Back in March I think it was, during a night out, we decided it'd be fun to have a camping holiday together and well, here we are."

"How about her past?" Zena asked, "You know, did she seem to bear a grudge against anyone or anything? Have a chip on her shoulder? You know the sort of thing I mean."

"Not really," said Hannah. "She never much mentioned her past other than to say she hated school."

"She told us about her parents though, didn't she?" Diane reminded them, "you know, how they'd split up after her dad had an affair."

Hetty's ears pricked up. "Really! Do you know any details?"

"A few," said Hannah, "but not many. Apparently, it went on for two or three months, the affair, that is, and when her mum found out she was furious and promptly filed for divorce despite Gretel's dad begging for forgiveness. After that the family home in Canterbury was sold and they all went their separate ways. Having seen an advert online for a flatmate in Reading, Gretel, who was eighteen at the time, was thankful to move miles away from her original home. She didn't want to go with her mother, you see, because she thought her behaviour was unreasonable and part blamed her for her dad's infidelity. Anyway, within twelve months her dad's health deteriorated, he lost his job and took to drink. Gretel kept in touch and he died a year or so ago."

"Yes," Diane agreed. "It wasn't something Gretel talked about much and she only told us one night when she'd had too much to drink."

"That's right, and because we knew it was a bitter subject we avoided talking about our own parents and family life because we didn't want to upset her," Hannah added.

Lottie, sitting beside Layton, placed her brandy and advocaat on the table. "Girls, I know it's a big ask, but do you have any idea who it was that her father had the affair with?"

The expression on the faces of Hannah and Suzy were blank.

"She never mentioned a name," said Diane, "but if I remember correctly the woman was a writer or something like that. You know, she could have been a journalist or even an auth…Oh, my goodness. How could we have been so blind? It must have been Shelley Sinclair."

178

Paul, leaning against the bar with Jed, spoke for the first time. "Good grief. I'm flabbergasted. So it looks as though you ladies were on the right track all along."

Hetty eyes twinkled, she nodded but thought it best not to speak.

Zena slipped to the bar and returned with three glasses of brandy. She handed one each to the girls. "Here, drink these. You're in shock and they will help."

They expressed their thanks.

"You know, with hindsight we ought to have suspected something. I mean, she was often bitter and quite scathing about people who seemed to be happy, wasn't she?" Suzy turned to Emma, sitting on a nearby table with Zac, "especially you, Em. She was two-faced too and dead jealous about your up and coming wedding."

"Now you come to mention it, that's very true," agreed Hannah, "Remember how green she went when you, Emma told us that your wedding reception was to be in the ballroom at Pentrillick House?"

"Absolutely," Suzy agreed, "and this afternoon when we were talking about the horrid fire, she said with a great grin on her face that it was a bit of a comedown going from having a wedding reception in a grand ballroom to a miserable tent. At the time we thought she was trying to be funny but now I reckon she meant it."

Happy Harper, hearing what was said raised his hand to speak, "Umm, it's just a thought but could she have started the fire this morning?"

"What!" gasped Hetty, "No, surely she'd not be that wicked."

Hannah shook her head. "No, I agree, I don't think she'd be that mean. On the other hand she didn't go running with us this morning. Said she wasn't feeling too good so we went without her."

"How long were you gone for?" Paul asked.

Suzy shrugged her shoulders. "An hour, hour and a half, maybe two. Not sure."

"Long enough for her to have driven to Pentrillick House and started the fire then," reasoned Lottie.

"That's why I asked," said Happy, "I saw her go out in the car this morning, you see. About five minutes after you girls left. I wondered why because it was too early to go shopping or anything like that."

"How long was she gone for?" Paul asked.

"Phew, umm, let's see. I went for a shower at half seven and she came back just minutes after I returned to my van. So I suppose, she was away for just over an hour."

"More than long enough to drive out there, start the fire and get back again then," calculated Paul.

"Does anyone know where and how the fire started?" Debbie asked.

"Tristan said they think it started in the ballroom," responded Emma, "but it's too early to say how."

Hetty caught sight of a collection tin on the bar for donations towards a new bicycle for Pickle. "Perhaps she's responsible for everything that's happened this summer then. I mean, it's just a thought and I don't remember seeing you there, but did you girls go to the fete?"

"Yes, we did," said Suzy, "We went with Harry, Jack and Jake, didn't we lads?"

Harry nodded. "Yes, Mum and Dad wanted us and me in particular to go and support it because they felt bad over the church not being able to use the pub field. We weren't there long. An hour, maybe more."

"And did Gretel by any chance leave you for any length of time?"

"Funny you should say that," said Hannah, "because we'd not been there long when she said she needed to go to the loo and nipped off, I assume into the care home. Why do you ask?"

"I'm thinking of Pickle's bike and the fact someone cut his brake cables with wire cutters."

Diane gasped. "Surely you don't think Gretel did that?"

"I don't know. That's why I'm asking."

Paul took over from Hetty. "Did she or any of you visit the white elephant stall?"

Hannah smiled. "White elephant stall. Whatever's that?"

"A bit like a jumble stall, only no clothes, just toys, kitchen stuff and so forth," said Lottie, "You know, odds and sods."

"And tools," Debbie added.

"Yes, yes we did. That's where the nice chap was selling stuff with a lady. The boat chap I mean. We went out with him for a trip along the coast last week. He's really funny."

"That's right," said Lottie, "Bernie and his wife, Veronica were manning it, and they are a smashing pair."

"Did you buy anything and what did you look at?" Paul asked.

"I bought half full bottle of my favourite perfume," said Diane, "It was a gift at seventy-five pence. I think I was the only one though."

"Yeah, I didn't buy anything," said Suzy, "Not there anyway."

"Nor me," said Hannah.

"I bought a leather belt," said Jack, "because I forgot to bring one with me and being skinny my jeans keep slipping down."

"How about Gretel?" Paul asked.

The colour drained from Suzy's face. "She didn't buy anything but she was looking at tools. Said she was hoping to find a tiny screw driver to tighten the loose arm of her sunglasses."

Chapter Twenty-Five

In police custody, Gretel Slater refused to co-operate and so was locked in a cell where they hoped by morning she would have changed her mind. Her fingerprints had been taken to see if there was a match with the disposable barbecue, but although the evidence pointed strongly in her direction at that point they were unable to establish a motive. However, in the early hours of Saturday morning, retired Detective Inspector Paul Fox phoned David Bray and told him of a possible motive having spoken to Gretel's friends.

The following morning, Gretel, realising that to deny her part in the death of the two cousins was futile because her fingerprints would inevitably match those taken from the disposable barbecue, decided to confess. In a recorded interview, she told Detective Inspector Bray and Detective Sergeant Caroline Stone that although she loathed Shelley Sinclair, she had never seen or met her prior to the holiday but knew of her because of the part she had played in the break-up of her parents' marriage. It was a shock therefore when she realised one of the two middle-aged women camping close by was none other than her nemesis, Shelley Sinclair.

Asked to tell of the events leading up to the evening of August 10th she explained how two days after they had arrived in Pentrillick, having realised who Shelley Sinclair was, she and the girls went out for a run. They followed the coastal path and growing in a valley by a wooden bridge, she spotted what she thought to be a hemlock. Knowing from her schooldays how deadly it was she took a picture of the plant to Google it later, as she was unsure because the flower heads had gone to seed and she knew hemlock and cow parsley looked very much alike. A few days later, having verified its identity, and having made up her mind to teach Ms Sinclair a lesson, she suggested but without giving a reason of course, that they took the same route again and this time she made sure that she was well behind the others. As she passed the hemlock with a tissue in her hand, she reached out and grabbed a handful of leaves. She then stuffed them into the pocket in her shorts. Later, when she was alone, she finely chopped the leaves, placed them in a plastic bag and knowing that the cousins usually had salad with their meals, awaited the chance to sprinkle them over Shelley Sinclair's dinner. This she achieved on the evening the local band were playing when Beatrice went to the bar for drinks and Shelley's attention was taken by the arrival of the American and his wife. It was while Shelley was distracted that she hurriedly told her friends she was going to the loo. As she crossed the bar she took a pinch of the shredded leaves from the bag and on passing the cousin's table subtly sprinkled it onto the salad while Shelley's head was turned. She didn't want Shelley to die; she just wanted to make her ill and ruin her holiday. For that reason she was horrified when she realised it was Beatrice who had eaten the leaves and much to her horror had consequently died. At the same time it made her even more angry and she blamed Shelley Sinclair, not only for the death of her father but Beatrice Cookson too.

A few days later, when she saw Shelley was intending to cook on a disposable barbecue, she made a plan to slip the aluminium tray, providing it was still hot, into her tent later that evening when they returned from the pub. Delighted that Shelley had the barbecue lit and held a glass of wine in her hand when they went out for a drink, she had high hopes that her plan would work. However, because they were later leaving the pub than she'd anticipated, she found that Shelley had been safety conscious and the barbecue was not only cold but full of water, thus would be ineffective. However, shortly after as she tried to sleep she heard the lads in the caravan come back from a day out and they had a barbecue too. She kept herself awake and then when they finally turned in for the night, crept out and found their still hot barbecue beneath the caravan steps. Taking care to make no noise, she slipped the hot tray inside Shelley's tent. She wasn't worried about waking the author because she was quietly snoring and the empty wine bottle by the bricks indicated she had drunk the lot hence should sleep soundly. After leaving the tent, she put Shelley's cold barbecue beneath the boy's caravan. But again she added, she didn't want Shelley Sinclair to die from carbon monoxide poisoning, she just wanted to make her sick and teach her a lesson.

"And while we're here. What about the fire?" Detective Inspector David Bray asked.

"Fire! I don't know anything about a fire."

"Come on. You were in the pub last night and I'm told everyone was talking about it."

"Oh, that fire," she shrugged her shoulders, "still know nothing about it."

The detective pointed to a large sticking plaster around the back of her hand. "Okay, so what happened there?"

"Oh that. I scratched it on a thorn of the hawthorn bush behind our wigwam. The stuff's deadly and ruined Suzy's swimsuit when she put it on there to dry."

For several minutes more she remained adamant that she could tell them nothing about the fire. That was until the Detective Sergeant Caroline Stone mentioned that she was seen leaving the campsite that morning and was gone for an hour. Realising she was already in deep water she muttered 'Oh well, I might as well be hung for a sheep as a lamb' and confessed. She told how she had broken a pane of glass in one of the windows hoping the glass would fall onto a chair beneath it and not make too much noise. She then lit a rag soaked in petrol and pushed it through the hole. It fell onto the chair and when she saw its upholstery was on fire, she ran back across the lawns to her car and returned to the campsite and took a shower to get rid of the smell of petrol. She was in the wigwam placing the sticking plaster over the cut she'd received from the jagged window glass when her friends arrived back fifteen minutes later.

"Care to tell us why?" said DS Stone, "Why on earth did you want to destroy Pentrillick House?"

"I didn't want to destroy it. I guessed there would be smoke alarms around the place, possibly sprinklers too and these historic places often have their alarms linked to the local fire stations. For that reason I didn't think too much damage would be done before the fire brigade arrived."

"But why start it at all?"

She hung her head. "I just wanted to mess up the ballroom. I was jealous, you see. Jealous that someone as ordinary as Emma Mannering could have a wedding reception in a lovely place like that. Jealous she had a family who loved her. Jealous she had a home of her own. Jealous she had a job she loved. It just seemed so unfair."

The DS felt a pang of pity. "And Percy Pickering's bicycle?"

"What!" she screamed, "Who the hell is Percy Pickering?"

The gentleman whose brake cables were cut at the fete."

"Well you can't pin that one on me because I didn't do it."

"But I suggest you did. What happened? Did you think he might have seen you slip the hemlock over the salad or was it because he might have seen you swap over the disposable barbecues?"

"Neither because it wasn't me. I bore no grudge against whatever you said his name was and never touched the poor bloke's bike."

Detective Sergeant Stone, cast a glance at DI David Bray and then gathered up the papers on the table. "We'll just have to wait then and see if there's a fingerprint match."

Gretel shrugged her shoulders. "Whatever."

Shortly after results of the fingerprints came back. Gretel's prints matched those on the disposable barbecue but to the surprise of DI Bray and DS Stone, did not match the unaccounted for prints on the wire cutters.

Because of Gretel's arrest and the fact that the four wigwam girls had travelled down to Cornwall in Gretel's car, they realised they had little choice other than to stay put over the Bank Holiday weekend while they made arrangements to get home. After various phone calls it was agreed that Hannah's brother would travel to Cornwall by train on the Monday, pick up the car and the girls and drive them home. This was agreed with Gretel's mother who wanted time to think before she herself visited Cornwall and her daughter with whom she seldom saw eye to eye.

Meanwhile, at The Old Lifeboat House, the Dexters were packing their bags ready to return home with every intention of calling at the hospital en route to visit Tristan and Samantha Liddicott-Treen before they were discharged. At the Crown and Anchor, Zena Marshall had already vacated her room and left the village.

On the camping field, Happy Harper, reluctant to leave, decided to stay for another day. This was fortuitous. For in the afternoon, Zac and Emma received yet more bad news via a phone call from their wedding photographer's wife. Her husband had been taken seriously ill and she was having to cancel all his bookings for at least the month of September. Hearing of their misfortune from Tess, while in the pub for his lunch, Happy promptly asked where Zac and Emma lived and then called on them at their home in Cobblestone Close to offer his services should they not already have found someone else.

Chapter Twenty-Six

Due to the Friday night drama and subsequent arrest of Gretel Salter, Bill had given no more thought to Norman's information regarding the comment made by Clarence the parrot in connection with his mother. However, on Sunday morning it sprang back to mind when someone at work made reference to a budding romance between two work colleagues. Hence when he returned home just after five, he went straight out to the garden and pulled leaves from a lettuce. After placing them in two small piles he searched for Tim who he found ambling around beneath the apple tree.

"I've a job for you young man. A very, very important job." He placed the tortoise down on the grass facing the lettuce leaves. Behind one pile was a piece of card saying 'yes' on the other a card saying 'no'. "Right Tim. I want to know if there's any truth in Clarence's claim that Layton loves me mum. So off you go."

Sandra, watching from the kitchen window, wondered what latest issue the poor tortoise was expected to foretell. After all it had become quite a habit with her husband which she found a little unnerving. When curiosity got the better of her she went outside to see.

"You and your tortoise," she chuckled, "You're as bad as your mum and aunt and their crystal ball," she sat down beside Bill on a garden bench, "So what are you hoping Tim will predict this time?"

Bill repeated his brief conversation with Norman on Friday evening.

"Really! But that's wonderful and wouldn't it be lovely if it's true and they were to marry?"

"What! Would it? Oh, I don't know. Let's see what Tim has to say first."

Patiently they waited for the tortoise to reach the lettuce leaves where much to Bill's surprise Tim opted for yes.

"Hmm," he mumbled. "I won't tackle Mum until I've heard what our Barbara thinks."

Sandra stood up. "I don't think you'll tackle her at all, William. She's perfectly capable of making decisions for herself and you must not interfere."

"Well, we'll see about that."

Shortly after, as pre-arranged, Barbara and Jed called in for a chat before dinner at the Pentrillick Hotel. No sooner were they through the door than Bill had acquainted them with the latest news.

"But that's wonderful," said Barbara, whose enthusiasm equalled Sandra's. "I think they make a really sweet couple."

"Do you really?" Bill was astonished. "I've never thought of them as a couple."

"Oh, I have ever since I clapped eyes on them both chatting away together. Remember I hadn't seen Mum for years so would see her in a different light to you and there's no doubt she positively shines when Layton is around."

"Does she?" Feeling dizzy, Bill sat down. "I don't know what to say or think, except that if they got together, what would Auntie Het do?"

"What! Auntie Het's as tough as old boots. She'll be fine."

"And don't forget Hetty spent years living alone before she retired and came to Cornwall with your mother," Sandra reminded him, "although I have to admit she's said many a time how much nicer it is to share a home with someone."

"Anyway, I don't see it as a problem," said Barbara. "If Auntie Het's lonely she can share a home with Paul because they're obviously the best of friends."

"Paul!" Bill gasped, "What Paul as in the ex-copper?"

"Well, of course that's who she means," said Sandra. "How many Pauls do you know?"

"Actually there are two at work. Paul Watkins and Paul Bradbury."

Sandra looked heavenwards. "Well it's hardly likely to be either of them, is it?"

Bill dug in his heels. "But what'd happen to Primrose Cottage? Mum and Auntie Het both love that house."

"I think we're jumping the gun a bit here," laughed Sandra. "At present no-one has hinted that things are about to change. Well, other than a parrot and a tortoise."

"Hmm," Barbara sat down in the middle of the couch beside her brother. "It's just a thought though, but if Mum and Auntie Het were to leave Primrose Cottage, to save a lot of hassle we could rent it from them or if they're willing, buy it even."

Bill frowned. "But you live in America so rather a long way to commute."

Barbara reached up to Jed's hand and pulled him down beside her. "We have some news, don't we, Jed?"

He nodded. "Yep."

"And?" Bill said.

"We're coming home," said Barbara: "thanks to Jackie, Jed has discovered that he not only has Cornish roots but that his ancestors came from West Cornwall and he's possibly a very distant relative to Mum and Auntie Het's friend, Kitty, although we doubt it. To be honest we love it here and over this last few weeks I've realised just how much I miss my family. My only family and I want to be nearer to you all."

Bill's face lit up. "Wow! That's wonderful but how will Jed get on not being a British citizen?"

"Oh, I'm sure we can work that out," said Barbara. "After all I have dual citizenship and as my husband I'm sure we'll get round it."

"I keep forgetting you're married," said Bill, "and that I have an American brother-in-law."

"So do I," agreed Sandra, "but what about work? What will you both do?"

"I don't think I'll have difficulty finding a job," said Barbara, "and to be honest I'd be quite happy doing anything."

Jed chuckled. "And I want to join your wonderful police force. That's if they'll have me."

"There's a real nip in the air," said Hetty, as she came in from the back garden after hanging out the washing on Bank Holiday Monday, "and a brisk easterly wind too so the washing should be dry in no time."

"Yes, summer's well and truly in its last throes. It'll be September on Thursday, so hopefully there won't be any more extremely hot weather again this year."

Hetty sat down at the table where Lottie had just placed two mugs of tea. "We'll be lost today not having to open up the charity shop. We haven't had a Monday off for ages."

"Actually we did, a few weeks back when we swapped days with Daisy and Maisie so we could meet Barbara and Jed at the station, but then we made up for it so yes, it's nice to have an extra day off."

"So what shall we do with it?"

Lottie shrugged her shoulders. "Don't know. Wedding preparations are under control and so our help's not needed there and we now know who was responsible for Shelley and Beatrice's deaths, so there's nothing more to look into there either."

"And we know it was Gretel who started the fire at Pentrillick House. So callous."

"Ah, there is one thing still to uncover and that's who tampered with Pickle's bike."

"I still think it was Gretel," said Hetty, "I know her prints weren't on the wire cutters but she could have worn gloves or held them with a tissue. Something like that."

"True, but for some reason I don't think it was her. In fact it was quite likely a local person who bore a grudge for some reason."

Hetty glanced at the calendar: "I wonder if there will be a quiz tonight. You know, with it being a Bank Holiday."

"Yes, there is. I remember seeing on the notice board that the prize money will be double this week because of the Bank Holiday."

"Right, the pub tonight then and it should be quite good anyway because James and Ella are going to present Pickle with his bike money now they've gone over five hundred pounds."

Pickle knew nothing about the collection to raise money for him to buy a new bicycle, put into action after Norman, having spoken to Pickle at Saltwater House, mentioned his dilemma to James and Ella in the pub one night. On the few occasions Pickle had been to the Crown and Anchor while the collection tin was in place, either James, Ella or a member of staff would quickly slip it away and hide it beneath the bar counter.

The collection tin was still on the counter when Hetty and Lottie arrived at the pub on Monday evening.

"We're leaving it there in case there are a few more wanting to donate," said Tess, "but as usual we'll whip it away when Pickle gets here."

"You're sure he'll be here then?" Lottie asked.

"Yes, he loves quizzes but to be on the safe side, Bernie and Veronica have already asked him to make up a team along with Norman."

"So when are you thinking of giving the money to him?" Hetty nodded her thanks as Tess placed two glasses of wine on the bar.

"After the quiz. While James is asking the questions, Ella will nip out the back, count it up and write out a cheque for the collected amount. Needless to say the change is useful for us to go in the till."

Standing next to the sisters was Joseph Baker who with his wife Mary was staying at Sea View Cottage.

"Excuse me for interrupting, but is this being collected for the poor chap who came off his bike on the day of the church fete?"

"That's right," said Tess, "Percy Pickering known to us all as Pickle."

"Then please let me make a small contribution." He pulled out his wallet and pushed a ten pound note into the slit. "I've a bicycle back home, which I've come off once or twice but never suffered any damage to either me or the bike, not like your poor Pickle did."

"That's very kind," said Tess, "Thank you."

Shortly after Hetty and Lottie had taken seats in the corner, Debbie and Kitty arrived. With them were their husbands, Gideon and Tommy.

"Excellent," said Lottie, as the ladies took their seats and the men went to the bar, "Six heads are better than four."

"That's what we thought," said Debbie, "We knew Layton and Paul were playing with Sid, Jude, and the girls from the pasty shop so decided to drag our better halves along as I should imagine the competition will be tight tonight with it being a Bank Holiday and double the prize money."

Paul arrived shortly after with Dolly, Sid, Eve and Jude. He waved as he sat and then turned away because Layton had just walked in the door.

"We have to beat them," hissed Hetty. "I'm sure Paul thinks we're a bit dim because of our tendency to solve

192

crimes, or not as the case might be, so we have to prove that actually we're really clever."

"Even if we're not," chuckled Debbie.

"Well if we don't get the answers right it'll be because James asked the wrong questions," reasoned Kitty, pragmatically, "It's as simple as that."

"However the ladies with the help of Tommy and Gideon did do well and to their great surprise they came first by a narrow margin. Paul, Layton, the pasty shop girls and their partners came a healthy third.

After the prize money was distributed, James asked for quiet and then on behalf of the pub's clientele he awarded Pickle a cheque for five hundred and forty-two pounds.

Pickle, clearly unaware that a collection had been made, was overwhelmed and before he had a chance to say anything, James assured him that the money was not charity, it was a gift, a gift to show goodwill and to help him replace something precious that was lost through no fault of his own. After which, Pickle graciously accepted the cheque and thanked everyone present. It was as he tucked the cheque inside his wallet that he noticed Joseph amongst the crowd clapping with enthusiasm. He frowned as a memory flashed across his mind. "Why do I feel I know you?"

Joseph laughed. "Could be because at the church fete we were both looking at plants or it might be because you nearly ran us down one drizzly night along the main street. You were on your bike and bumped against us as we were crossing the road to get to Sea View Cottage."

"Ah, yes, I remember you at the fete but only vaguely recall knocking into you. Did I stop? I just don't remember."

"No, but you shouted 'sorry mate' as you pedalled away."

"Whoops, hope you were alright."

"Yes, no harm done."

It was Bernie's turn to frown. He addressed Joseph. "I'm not accusing you but at the fete you were looking at tools. I remember now because you told me you were a carpenter."

"And so I was. Well, until I retired, that is."

"Hmm, interesting, but at some point during that afternoon the wire cutters disappeared and then Pickle's brake cables were snipped."

All chattering in the bar halted as everyone attempted to listen.

Joseph held up his hands. "Well it wasn't me. It'd take a lot more than being knocked into by a bike to make me want to do someone harm. And to be honest, it amused me anyway because Pickle here was obviously three sheets to the wind."

"Hey! No. If it's the night I think it might have been I was stone cold sober and on my way home having been down to Long Rock helping a mate put up a plasterboard ceiling. I seldom bring my bike to the pub as I don't like to drink and ride and if I was a bit wobbly it was because the light drizzle on my specs was making visibility a challenge."

"Ah! In that case I beg your pardon, but as I've already said I know nothing about cutting brake cables other than what I've heard said in here. What's more, being a cyclist, I'd never do such a thing."

"No, I don't think you would," Bernie offered Joseph his hand to shake. "Sorry if I offended you, mate."

"Oh, say no more. I'd have probably thought the same in your shoes."

Looking uncomfortable, Mary grabbed Joseph's arm. "Come on, love, let's go now."

"What. No," he shook his arm free, "Why on earth should we go now? It's only half nine and there's nothing on the telly tonight."

Mary's shoulders slumped; she looked deflated. Veronica standing by her husband and puzzled by Mary's sudden lack of command, gently reached out and touched her arm. "Are you alright? You look awfully pale."

"Yes. No. Actually, I feel sick." She hung her head, "And that's because it was me. I cut the brake cables and I feel really ashamed now."

Joseph's jaw dropped. "You did what! But why?"

"Because he hit us. The bike's handle bar tugged at your pocket and tore it, that's why. And I thought that you, Pickle, should have stopped and apologised. Revenge seemed justified when I did it but not now and I'm truly sorry."

"And so you should," snapped Joseph.

Mary bit her bottom lip. "Are you going to press charges, Pickle?"

"Ow, I dunno." A cheeky smile turned into a chuckle, "No, of course I'm not. As far as I'm concerned it's six of one and half a dozen of the other."

"That's very gracious of you, sir," said Joseph, "but since the police already have it on their books we'll pop along and explain. I'm sure that with Mary being an old dear she'll get away with a caution. At least I hope so."

Mary looked relieved. "Thank you and please believe me when I say I never intended you to get hurt or for your bike to get damaged. I just wanted you to fall off. I calculated you'd realise the brakes were gone well before you reached the bottom of the road, you see. And that you'd steer into the hedge in order to stop."

"I think these good people here deserve a proper explanation, Mary, so please tell them, and me for that matter, just how you went about sabotaging this poor chap's bike."

"It wasn't premeditated or anything like that. In fact the thought didn't cross my mind until I saw you, Pickle, ride into the care home grounds and leave your bike by the hedge. At the time, Joseph and I were heading to the tea tent and because the place was busy and the ladies there were overstretched, I offered to help for a while and was there for about half an hour. After leaving them to it, I wandered around and on the white elephant stall I saw a very nice vase. I also saw the wire cutters and that's when the thought of revenge popped through my mind. It actually made me giggle. I didn't want to buy the cutters though in case the people on the stall remembered who'd bought them. So I bought the vase and while my change was being sorted, I slipped the cutters into the vase and then when my change was proffered I said to keep it and add it to funds. That way, I reasoned it'd cover the cost of the cutters I'd taken. I then walked over towards the bike, snipped the brake wires and returned the cutters to the vase. After finding you Joseph, we spent another half hour there and then left. As we reached the bottom of the hill we saw two men standing near to what looked like a body in a ditch and to my horror I realised who it was. Joseph, having first aid knowledge, handed me his bag of purchases and ran off down the road to see if he could help at all and got there just as the ambulance arrived. While he was gone I took the cutters from the vase and chucked them over the hedge. Of course as soon as I did it I realised my fingerprints would be on them but I assured myself I'd be safe as the police would have no reason to suspect me. It never occurred to me they might link it to the death of the two ladies whom we never met, hence I was relieved when the culprit of those deaths was caught and the investigation into the bike incident by the police took a back shelf."

After shaking hands, Joseph bought Pickle a drink and they sat down at a table together along with Mary. By the end of the evening you'd have thought they were lifelong friends.

Chapter Twenty-Seven

"No, no, no," Hetty's piercing cry rang through the house on Tuesday morning.

Lottie about to make mugs of tea ran in from the kitchen, kettle still in her hands. "Whatever's the matter?"

Hetty was seated on the couch waving her arms at the television set. "I've just seen the weather and there's rain forecast for Saturday."

Lottie's shoulders slumped. "Is that all? I thought something was seriously wrong."

"This is serious. Low pressure is setting in at the weekend. It's likely to be windy too. What a nightmare."

"Well, Zac and Emma won't be the first couple to have inclement weather on their wedding day and they won't be the last either. We'll just have to put up with whatever is thrown at us and make the best of it."

"Why are you always so positive?"

"Because sometimes it's the only way to be," Lottie turned towards the doorway. "I'll get back to making the tea now that bit of drama is over." And shaking her head she returned to the kitchen.

As August gave way to September so the excitement of the impending wedding grew despite the poor weather forecast. On Thursday September the first, Zac's old school friend, Dodge arrived from Northamptonshire to take up the role of best man. He was greeted warmly by Zac and Emma at their home in Cobblestone Close where he was to be a guest. Meanwhile, at the Crown and Anchor, the marquee from Pentrillick House had arrived and was being erected on the field.

The following day, more friends and relations arrived and booked into their chosen accommodation, namely, the Crown and Anchor, Tuzzy-Muzzy guest house and the Pentrillick Hotel.

The night before the wedding, Zac and Dodge, were preparing for a trip to the Crown and Anchor where they were to meet up with Zac's friend, Kyle. Shortly after as Emma left to return to her parents' home for the evening, Dodge assured her, hand on heart, that none of them would over indulge. Emma squeezed his hand and thanked him sincerely. She felt quite emotional. The wedding date had changed several times over the past two years and she prayed there would be no last minute hitches.

Zac, Kyle and Dodge were as good as the best man's word. None had more than three pints and Zac and Dodge were back at Cobblestone Close well before James rang last orders. However, things might have been different had Zac not been conscious of the watchful eyes of his mother, Aunt Barbara, his grandmother and his Great Auntie Hetty. But the ladies didn't stay late either as they wanted to ensure a good night's sleep before the big day.

As predicted, September the third dawned grey and dull, but not one to dwell on the negative, Emma told her parents, without self-pity, that the gardens needed the ensuing rain and nothing would dampen her spirit.

The wedding was due to take place at two o'clock and at midday, bridesmaids, Vicki and Kate arrived at the Mannering family home beneath dripping umbrellas. Emma's younger sister, Claire, also a bridesmaid, was already in situ as being in her mid-teens she still lived with her parents.

In the marquee caterers were busy; the tables were already dressed having been decorated the previous day along with floral displays on pedestals. Just after midday, Dolly and Eve from the pasty shop arrived with the wedding cake. Both ladies had done cake decorating as part of their studies when much younger but it was something neither had pursued. However, after talking with Emma and her mother about extending the business and going into celebration cake making, they offered to make a wedding cake but only charge for ingredients for their initial project. Emma and her mother agreed it was an offer not to be sneezed at but all the same they intended to drop a considerable sum of money into an envelope to give to the ladies after the wedding as a thank you present.

From his camper van, Happy Harper looked at the grey skies and wondered if there might be a break in the clouds as the wedding party left the church or if there would be a heavy shower thus making photography impossible. It was a dilemma he had faced many times over the years and as usual he would have to play it by ear. As he changed into an outfit bought specially for the occasion, the clothes with him being far too casual, his thoughts drifted to Shelley and Beatrice. Already their presence in the village was becoming a distant memory. "Live for today because tomorrow may never come," he muttered.

At three minutes to two when Emma and her father arrived at the church, the rain had eased a little but the wind had freshened. Greeted by Vicar Sam in the church porch, Emma heaved a sigh of relief on hearing that Zac and Dodge were standing by the chancel step, eagerly awaiting her arrival. And it was from that step that Zac drew in a deep breath as the girl he had first clapped eyes on as she waitressed in a café during her student days back in 2016, stepped towards him a huge smile on her face.

To the delight of Happy Harper, the rain had stopped when the couple emerged from the church and Vicar Sam knowing the importance of wedding pictures asked for volunteers to carry out a large rug from the vestry to lay outside the church porch to protect dresses and shoes. And as Happy took the first picture the sun briefly peeped out from behind a dark cloud. However, by the time the party were ready to leave for the Crown and Anchor's field, it was drizzling again.

Inside the marquee, Happy took pictures of the bridal party and guests, along with the wedding cake on top of which someone had slipped a cocktail umbrella between the sugar paste figures of the bride and groom.

Zac and Emma left their guests just after six for the drive to Bristol where they had a hotel room booked to enable them to access the airport early on Sunday morning for their flight to Paphos. By then the evening guests had already arrived and a party in the marquee was in full swing with local band Treacle Toffee playing, to be followed by a disco. Dodge having said goodbye to his old friend was then taken under the wings of the twins who had known him for as long as they could remember.

As the evening wore on, the music increased in volume and so did the chatter of the party-goers. Several people made their way home or to their accommodation and those not wanting a premature end to the day drifted off into the pub where things were a little quieter. All in all the day was a huge success, despite the weather, and one that locals felt they would remember for a very long time.

On Tuesday morning, Hetty and Lottie drove Barbara and Jed to Penzance station for the hired car they had used during their stay had been returned the previous day. It was a tearful farewell but Barbara assured them it was merely adieu for they would be back for good once everything was settled back in the States.

The following two days carried on as normal but then on Thursday the eighth of September the world it seemed stood still. Lottie and Hetty had spent much of the afternoon in the garden tidying it up ready for winter. It was a surprise therefore when they sat down with cups of tea in the living room and switched on the six o'clock news. Doctors were seriously concerned about Queen Elizabeth's health and family members were making their way to Balmoral in Scotland where she had been staying for several weeks. The sisters sat and watched in silence and disbelief; it wasn't until the news of her death was broadcast shortly after that both found their voices.

For the next eleven days talk in the village was of little else other than the loss of the UK's longest serving monarch. And on September the nineteenth, the same group assembled at Saltwater House to watch the funeral as had watched the Platinum Jubilee concert from Buckingham Palace just three months previously. When coverage finished Layton told his friends that on Saturday he would be seventy-one. He had had a word with James and Ella and they had agreed to lay on a buffet so they could get together to celebrate. Everyone agreed that after the sombre mood of late, reason to celebrate would be very welcome.

The following evening, Hetty sat alone watching the television; Lottie was out with Layton dining at their favourite retro restaurant. Hetty was switching off the television set when her sister arrived home.

"Don't go yet, Het," said Lottie, seeing Hetty pick up her book and reading glasses meaning she was off to bed, "there's something I need to tell you."

Hetty sat back down much aware of the twinkle in her sister's eyes and suddenly she knew what Lottie was about to say.

"Layton has asked me to marry him and I've said yes."

On Thursday morning, Hetty sat alone on one of the benches on the seafront while Albert ran back and forth along the beach chasing gulls and wrestling with seaweed. Lottie and Layton had gone shopping to buy an engagement ring to replace the one bought for her many years ago by her late husband, Hugh, which now reposed on her right hand along with her wedding ring.

Hetty wasn't one to wallow in self-pity, but sitting there alone listening to the gentle rhythm of the waves made her feel melancholy. Everything was about to change and Hetty didn't much care for change. As the first tear trickled down her cheek she heard a familiar voice from behind.

"I thought I might find you here," Paul sat down by her side.

Feeling slightly embarrassed, Hetty quickly brushed away her tear. "How come?"

"Because I was sitting by the window strumming my guitar when I saw you go by, all alone and looking forlorn."

"I'm not forlorn."

"No? Why the tears then?"

"Because, because…"

"Because Lottie's going to marry Layton."

"You know?"

"Yes, he told me yesterday in confidence while we were playing golf that he intended to ask her and this morning he rang to say she'd said yes. He sounded extremely happy."

"I'm so glad. Really I am."

"You don't look it."

Hetty sighed. "I'm being foolish, aren't I? I mean, I spent years living alone so I'll just have to get used to being on my own again. The daft thing is and I know it's silly, but towards the end of last year I said that 2022 would be the best year ever and I've tried to pretend it is but it's not, is it? I mean, there's the dreadful situation in Ukraine, energy prices are bonkers, the cost of living is sky-high, Pentrillick House has been damaged by fire, we've had two murders in the village, we've lost The Queen and now I'm to lose Lottie too."

Paul placed his arm around Hetty's shoulder. "There is a solution to your dilemma and I'm sure it would work out well. I've given it a lot of thought and you could come and live with me."

Thinking he was joking, Hetty laughed but then she saw the look on his face said otherwise.

"I mean it, Het. Nothing would delight me more than you sharing my home with me or better still, you agreeing to be my wife." He looked up as Albert having spotted him came hurtling across the beach barking with tail wagging. Paul chuckled. "I think Albert would approve."

Saturday dawned damp and drizzly but by lunchtime it was bright and sunny. From the kitchen window Hetty, washing the dishes, watched Lottie singing as she hung out the washing. Hetty smiled. It was good to see her sister happy and no longer did she worry about her own destiny. Lottie, when told, had welcomed the idea of Paul's proposal, but said that it was a decision that only Hetty could make. Although Hetty knew she was right it didn't help one way or another, but she still had time because Paul had told her to think about it. Meanwhile, it was Layton's birthday and they had the celebrations to look forward to.

Amongst the gathering at the Crown and Anchor were Hetty and Lottie's next door neighbours, Detective Inspector David Bray and his partner, Margot. After a few drinks, Hetty found herself next to David as they helped themselves to buffet food in the dining room.

"I've been meaning to ask you for some time what the outcome was with the Mary and Pickle's bike incident. Do you know?"

"Yes, as anticipated she got off with a caution. She was very remorseful and apologetic and it was quite obvious she hadn't thought her actions through. It's a lesson to us all though – act in haste and repent at leisure."

Hetty winced, recalling Paul saying the same thing to her regarding their probing into the deaths of the two cousins.

"Since you're here," David waved a cocktail sausage on a stick. "Do you mind if I ask you a question?"

Hetty was surprised. "Err, no, I don't see why not."

"Well, a few weeks back I had reason to go over to Helston nick and while there from an upstairs window I saw you and Kitty Thomas taking turns to loiter outside in the street. But not only were you loitering but you kept changing your outfits. I've tried to fathom out what you might have been up to but am none the wiser."

"Ah, I see, well, umm…" Hetty felt her face flush with embarrassment but decided as she had nothing to lose she might as well tell the truth.

David slowly nodded his head. "I see, well, that sort of makes sense and Paul did warn me of your inquisitive nature."

"Yes, I'm sure he did, but how did you know it was us? I thought our changes of outfit were pretty convincing."

A huge smile crossed the DI's face. "It was the leggings, Hetty. You changed your tops and hats but not the leggings and you're the only person I know who wears brightly coloured floral ones."

At half past nine after the empty buffet plates were cleared away, Layton stood up and gave a little cough. "I, we, have a little announcement to make." He reached down and took Lottie's hand, "For those of you that don't yet know, Lottie and I are to be married and I'm the proudest and happiest man in the world."

Hetty, knew of course but had vowed not to tell anyone. Nevertheless, she watched with a tear in her eyes as people congratulated the couple and drinks flowed. It was good to see Lottie so happy. Seven years ago she had taken the loss of her husband very hard and Hetty having known Hugh well was confident he would very much approve of her sister's husband to be.

Debbie was in shock. "I knew they were close but didn't see this coming. What will you do, Het? Will you be alright on your own?"

"Oh, I'm sure I'll manage. Besides, Lottie won't be far away and I don't doubt you and Kitty will still be frequent visitors."

Paul was quick to join the conversation: "Or as I said the other day you could move in with me, Het. In fact I've given it a lot more thought and there's no need for us to marry if you'd rather not." He took her hand, "I'll let you into a little secret. Shortly before my late wife died she made me promise to find someone else because she couldn't bear the thought of me being all alone. She suggested that I find someone, who after years of solving crimes, many grim, would make me laugh. Make me happy. Make me smile. You fit that bill, Het and I know she would have loved you, as do I. What's more, I'd love your company and it seems daft for us both to be on our own."

"Oh, that's so sweet," gushed Debbie, "you must do it, Het. Marry Paul, that is. I would if I was in your position."

"Would you now," laughed Gideon.

Debbie slapped her husband's arm lovingly: "You know what I mean."

Hetty shook her head. "It's a lovely idea and thank you for asking, Paul, but I've given it a lot of thought and I'm just too old. You need to find someone your own age or better still someone younger than you. You're a fine looking man with years ahead of you and I'm sure there would be lots of women who'd be better suited than me." She looked down at the lines on her hands, "Being ten years older than you is just too much."

"Rubbish," scoffed Debbie, "Ten years is nothing. President Macron is twenty-four years younger than his wife, Brigitte, and they seem very happy."

"And you don't look a day over fifty-five anyway," added Gideon.

"You old flatterer," laughed Hetty, "Anyway, let me sleep on it for another day or two. It's been a very long and eventful summer and I don't want to make any rash decisions."

On Monday morning, Hetty and Lottie opened up the charity shop as usual. The day before they had talked of little else other than weddings and how much they were looking forward to Barbara and Jed leaving the States and joining the family in Cornwall. However, Lottie, who since the engagement had spoken with her daughter on the phone, didn't mention the muted idea that if both sisters were to vacate Primrose Cottage, Barbara and Jed would love to make it their home; the reason being she didn't want to put pressure on her sister. And while Hetty was pleased about the up and coming move, it never occurred to her to ask where Barbara and Jed planned to live.

Shortly before lunch as dark clouds gathered overhead, Debbie arrived blown in by a brisk north westerly wind. "Put the kettle on, ladies, we need to talk."

Hetty frowned. "I hope you're not going to start nagging me."

"Me, nag, of course not. Gentle persuasion is more in my line."

"Whoops. I'll make tea." Eager to avoid minor discord, Lottie slipped into the stockroom and reached for the kettle.

Hetty slumped down on a stool behind the counter. "Oh, Debbie, I don't know what to do. Part of me loves the idea of living with Paul. Marrying him even. We get on really, really well and I can't imagine him not being in my life. On the other hand, I really do feel that he would be better off with someone younger. And then there's his daughters. I'm too old to be a step-mum."

"Will you stop saying you're too old. You're the same age as me and I don't do old. As for Paul's daughters; they're both in their thirties and live up-country so your role as step-mum would be very limited indeed."

"Is she still making excuses?" Lottie emerged with a tray and then placed three mugs of tea on the counter.

"Yes, and I'm having none of it. You Hetty Tonkins are very stubborn."

Lottie sat down. "She always has been. Our dad was the same. Mind you, I wouldn't have her any other way."

Hetty glanced towards the windows. "Getting really dark out there and looks like rain."

"Don't try to change the subject," Debbie picked up her mug of tea and nodded towards the end of the counter. "How about you consult the crystal ball. It seems to know a thing or two."

Hetty actually raised a smile. "Okay but I don't really see how it will be helpful."

"Depends what you ask it, I suppose," reasoned Lottie, "but then it only need be a simple question such as should I or should I not marry Paul Fox."

Debbie nodded emphatically. "I absolutely agree and whatever it comes up with, whether it's positive or negative, we'll then let the subject drop, won't we, Lottie?"

With fingers crossed behind her back, Lottie agreed.

Hetty sighed, "Anything for a quiet life." With little enthusiasm, she stood up and closed her eyes.

"Stop," commanded Debbie. "Do it properly, Het, and put a curtain over your head so you look the part."

Hetty groaned, "If you say so." From a coat hanger she took a floral curtain, folded it in two and placed it over her dyed brown hair. Checking that her headdress met with the approval of her sister and Debbie, she then waved her hands slowly and thoughtfully over the crystal ball and asked if she should or should not marry Paul Fox. On opening them she gazed in anticipation to see what, if anything, shone from inside the glass orb. She gasped, for to her surprise, Paul himself looked her in the eye and smiled. While in two minds whether to tell the truth to her onlookers, Sid's words suddenly came back to her. *'You'll find when you look into a crystal ball, you see what you want to see.'*

A huge smile crossed Hetty's face. "I know the answer, girls. This frolicsome piece of glass has made up my mind and if the offer still stands, I shall marry Paul."

Epilogue

On Saturday, December the 31st, the last day of 2022, at the parish church in Pentrillick, guests congregated for a double wedding. By the chancel step, Vicar Sam who was to perform the ceremony, chatted to the grooms both smartly dressed in grey suits. Meanwhile, at Primrose Cottage, the twin sisters for the first time in many years had chosen to wear identical outfits; cream satin, midi-length, long-sleeved dresses, pink feather boas, pink and cream fascinators and cream coloured shoes. Each carried a bouquet of cream and pink carnations.

At ten minutes to three they left the house and their next door neighbour, David Bray, drove them to the church in his BMW. Waiting for them in the porch was Bill, who had agreed to give the sisters away.

"Well, this is it," said Hetty, her voice full of emotion, "The end of an era."

"And the beginning of a new one," Lottie squeezed her sister's hand, "Goodbye Miss Tonkins and good luck."

"Goodbye, Mrs Burton."

Bill folded him arms. "Listen to you two. Anyone would think you're never going to see each other again."

"Shush, Bill. Het and I are just saying goodbye to our old selves. We go back a long way."

As she spoke, Vicar Sam appeared. "Ah, you're here and looking lovely. All ready."

"As ready as we'll ever be," said Lottie.

"Yes," chuckled Bill, "time to give these two away."

Hetty frowned. "Would I be right in thinking you'll be glad to get rid of us?"

"No comment."

Bill felt himself nudged on both sides.

The wedding was meant to be a quiet affair with just a handful of guests; family and close friends for the ceremony and reception and then a free-for-all in the evening to celebrate the weddings and welcome in the New Year. However, when the sisters, either side of Bill, stepped into the church, they were overwhelmed to see every pew crammed with well-wishers leaving standing room only.

After the ceremony and pictures were taken beneath the grey clouds, the two couples made their way towards the lichgate where guests showered them with dried rose petals. The newly-weds then made their way to the Crown and Anchor for the reception in the dining room, where the grooms made speeches and toasts were made to absent friends.

As the evening wore on, Layton's sister, down for the wedding, left the Crown and Anchor for Saltwater House. Julia, a retired vet, who enjoyed peace and quiet, was happy to forgo the inevitable merrymaking and spend the evening in the company of Clarence and George, who earlier in the day had been joined by Albert so that he would not be left alone at Primrose Cottage.

As people mingled inside the busy pub, Tommy Thomas, Gideon Elms, Layton Wolf and Paul Fox stood by the piano chatting.

"Do you think they'll settle down now they're married?" Gideon asked. "I know they've both made New Year resolutions not to be busybodies anymore but even the most well-meaning vows seldom get past the end of January."

"I can't see it myself," said Tommy, "I've known them since the day they arrived here and I have to admit there's not been a dull day since, and they've certainly brightened up Kitty's life."

"I suppose we ought to go and join them," said Paul, "and make sure they're not plotting anything."

Around a table by a Christmas tree sat their four wives.

"Right, up you all get," said Tommy, "then we'll push some tables together."

Sid on the next table stood up. "Have our one as well, in fact and let's make one enormous table."

James, Ella, Jackie and Tess, watched in amusement from behind the bar as all square and oblong tables were carried and pushed together to make a huge rectangle.

"Perfect," said Layton, "now everyone grab a chair."

Thirty-six people sat down while others watched in amusement.

"This is like being at a Number 10 Cabinet meeting," chuckled Debbie, "although I think their table is oval."

"It's boat shaped," corrected Gideon, "so nearly right."

"Well, if this is a cabinet meeting, who's going to be PM?" Bill asked.

Hetty raised her hand. "Me. I'm in the right spot on the correct side. We'll pretend the bar is the fireplace."

"No, no, please not another female PM."

Sid raised his hands to protect his face as several cardboard beer mats flew in his direction. "Okay, I give up. Hetty can be PM just for tonight."

"What shall we discuss?" Sandra asked.

"Whatever comes into our heads," said Norman.

Pickle groaned. "As long as it's not politics."

"I'm with you there," Layton stood up. "But before we discuss anything we need our glasses topped up." He nodded to James who opened six bottles of wine, three red and three white. When glasses were full and bottles empty, he looked around the table. "Who's going first?"

"Me," said Kitty, "I have a question for the PM." She looked in Hetty's direction, "Prime Minister, do you think that now you're married you will settle down? I mean, will you really not endeavour to solve anymore murders, mysteries, crimes and what have you, should they arise?"

211

"Thank you Home Secretary, that is my New Year resolution and therefore should any criminal activity occur in the ensuing years then I/we shall leave solving said crimes to our excellent police force. Having said that I'm pretty sure there won't be any more mysteries. Not ones to entice us to poke our noses into anyway."

Debbie gasped. "Really! How do you know that, Het? I mean Prime Minister."

"Because the crystal ball said so." She took Paul's hand and squeezed it, "I asked that question, you see before I left work yesterday. Well, not in as many words. What I actually asked was, what I'd be doing in 2023, and when I looked into the ball I saw myself wearing a floral pinny, flicking a feather duster and being a housewife. I've never been a housewife before."

Debbie's jaw dropped. Was Hetty speaking tongue in cheek? Before she had a chance to find out, James switched on the radio and called out, "Two minutes to midnight."

Everyone around the tables then jumped up and stood behind their chairs; others in the bar joined them along with James, Ella, Tess and Jackie, taking a ten minute break. With crossed arms and linked hands, as the last bong of midnight chimed, they all sang Auld Lang Syne.

After lots of kissing, hugging and *bonhomie*, they all went outside to watch fireworks on the pub's field, administered by Sid and Bernie.

As they made their way back indoors, Lottie clasped Hetty's arm. "Thank you, Het."

"For what?"

"For suggesting we move here. For bringing me happiness after losing Hugh. For giving me a purpose in life. For being you."

"You old softie," Hetty gave Lottie a hug.

Debbie suddenly appeared in the doorway. "Come on you two dawdlers. Kitty is sitting at the piano and we're all going to do the conga snake dance."

"Coming," Hetty turned to her sister. "Happy New Year, Mrs Wolf."

"And a happy New Year to you, Mrs Fox."

With arms linked and heads held high, the sisters then followed Debbie indoors, into a new life, a new year and a new adventure.

THE END

Printed in Great Britain
by Amazon

23228305R00126